OPERATION: HIVE STRIKE

ERIC S. BROWN

SEVERED PRESS
HOBART TASMANIA

OPERATION: HIVE STRIKE

OPERATION: HIVE STRIKE!

The USS *Hellbringer* dropped out of Void space into the Wycarri system. In its hold, the battalion of colonial infantry troopers who would soon be dropping onto Wycarri Prime, the system's sole occupied planet, met for their various mission briefings. The battalion was broken up into platoons for the briefings. There was a total of eighteen platoons further broken down into ninety squads, each squad consisting for five to six troopers. Lieutenant Colonel Lyle was in overall command. He wasn't present for any of the briefings, however, as he was busy going over last minute details of the battalion's drop with the *Hellbringer*'s captain, Lewis. He had delegated out the briefings to the C.O. of each platoon who had been briefed earlier during the *Hellbringer*'s flight to the system.

The Wycarri system was home to the Mechi. The Earth Republic and the Mechi had been at war for just over six standard Earth months now. It was the hope of the Republic's higher powers that by striking at the heart of the Mechi domain, the war could be ended quickly. It was a risky gamble but one worth taking if it worked. Lieutenant Colonel Lyle's battalion had been assembled for the best of the best the Earth Republic's military had at its disposal. Unlike most battalions in the Earth Republic's service, Lyle's was comprised of a ratio of nine combat drop veterans to each green recruit among its ranks. And those recruits were all top of their various classes. What they lacked in field experience, they made up for in raw potential. The strike against

Wycarri Prime had been planned down to the smallest details. The entire battalion would touch down, via dropships, simultaneously, though spread out around the planet's capital city and primary spaceport. The objectives were to take out the spaceport and cause as much damage as possible to the city. The idea behind it all was a simple one, something along the lines of a basic "shock and awe" strategy. The intent was to show the Mechi that nowhere in their domain was safe from the Earth Republic's reach, and that if the Mechi persisted in their war against the Republic, they would pay dearly, even on the home front, for doing so.

Overall, the Mechi were inferior to the Earth Republic in technology. Their ships were slower and crude, basically heavily armored hulls, that relied mainly on their ability to take massive damage for long enough periods to destroy whatever vessels engaged them. Their sensor suites were substandard compared to even the most basic Earth Republic ships. It was an edge that the Republic hoped to exploit with this strike on Wycarri Prime. The *Hellbringer*'s limited cloaking tech would keep her from being detected until the very moment she emerged from Void space on a course for Wycarri Prime and her speed would do the rest. She would be through the ship's patrolling the system and in orbit around the Mechi's homeworld before any force capable of truly engaging her or keeping her at bay could stop her. Once in orbit, she would deploy Lieutenant Colonel Lyle's ground forces via dropships and bug out. The *Hellbringer*, it was believed, should be able to use her speed to escape any sort of serious engagement with in-system Wycarri forces and withdraw, jumping back into

Void space, under cloak, until such time as an extraction for the Lieutenant Colonel's ground forces was needed.

Sergeant Major Frank Wilson took on the job of briefing Alpha Platoon in Lieutenant Colonel Lyle's absence. Wilson wasn't a big man, but he was burly and rugged. His voice boomed as he addressed the soldiers of Alpha Platoon's squads. They were designated squads one through five; Beta Platoons were designated six through ten. Though the numbering of the squads continued on throughout the battalion, only the first two platoons took Greek numbers as their call signs. The rest of the platoons bore actual names such as The Butcher Dogs, The Nightmares, Ravenhead, etc.

"So here's the deal," Sergeant Major Wilson barked. "Everything's about to go pear-shaped. Just accept it. It's gonna happen. No op. ever runs exactly as it was planned. Each platoon in this battalion has a specific objective ranging from taking out disabling the planet's primary comm. and power girds to blowing the hell out of the planet's primary spaceport and whatever ships are docked there. Being Alpha Platoon, the comm. grid is our job. You can bet it'll be guarded by some of the nastiest Mechi they have down there. We will likely find ourselves outnumbered and outgunned. We'll have surprise on our side though, and as long as we keep pushing and pressing our initiative, we should be able to reach our target and take it out with only minimal casualties."

Second Lieutenant Fisher shot up a hand with a wry grin spread across his lips. "Define minimal."

Sergeant Major Wilson glared at him. "Stow it, Fisher," he growled and got back to business.

"The way out is going to be a hell of a lot hotter than the way in," Sergeant Major Wilson continued. "Every other platoon will be leaving one to two squads to protect the *Hellbringer*'s dropships. In addition, five full platoons will have the job of taking out any Mechi armor or nearby heavy weapons that might be brought to bear on them. You can thank whatever god or gods you pray to that we won't be among those poor bastards. As soon as our objective is achieved, we'll be returning to the dropships and bugging the frag out."

"What about Mechi fighters?" someone else asked, "Won't the dropships be vulnerable to them as we're bugging out?"

Sergeant Major Wilson sighed. "If the platoons assigned to taking out the spaceport do their job, the number of Mechi fighters able to get into the air will be limited at best. The *Hellbringer* herself should have returned to orbit around the planet by then for our extraction. Her fighters will join up with the dropships and see us home."

The members of Alpha Platoon were quiet as Sergeant Major Wilson finished. Just looking at them, he could see that most if, not all of them, were sharp enough to figure out just how small the odds were of any of them making it off Wycarri Prime alive. The smallest of missteps could cost the bulk of them their lives or worse, leave them stranded on the enemy's homeworld.

"Dismissed!" Sergeant Major Wilson shouted. "Get to your assigned dropships! It's time to kill some bugs!"

****

Corporal Wallace had strapped into place aboard Dropship 17. Strands of her fiery red hair poked out from underneath her helmet despite the short, bob-cut of her hair. Her intense green eyes scanned over the faces of the soldiers around her. The expressions she saw ranged from the outright yawns of veterans to the stark terror in the eyes of a newbie who was strapped into next to her.

She produced a lighter from one of the pockets of her vest and began to flip its top open and closed. Each time she flicked the lighter open, a bright flame of yellow and orange sprang into existence. Watching the flame brought her comfort. Wallace was well aware of how the other members of her squad felt about her. This was only her third combat drop, but her first two were already close to legendary status among the rank and file of the battalion. She was the only surviving member of her squad from both of those drops. While the officers above her had seen her survival as something to be rewarded and promoted her to the rank of corporal, the stories of those two drops scared the holy crap out of the soldiers she would be commanding on this one. Behind her back, she often heard the whispers of nicknames given to her like "Firedancer" or "Flame Lady."

"Ma'am," the sickly looking newbie to her called out, "would you mind not doing that?"

He gestured at her lighter.

Wallace laughed. "It's Loeb, right?"

"What?" the newbie was stunned. It took him a second to answer. "Yes, ma'am," he grunted at last. "Private First Class Loeb, ma'am."

Wallace continued flicking the lighter. "And what if I do mind, Loeb?" She grinned at him, her lips part in an almost feral way that showed the slightest hint of her white teeth.

Loeb swallowed hard, though she couldn't tell if it was in response to her question or merely him trying not to be sick. Most folks were on their first drop. Either way, he shut up and turned his eyes away from her.

Wallace chuckled quietly to herself as she continued to flick her lighter open and closed. Almost everyone in the infantry had some type of good luck charm or nervous tick that defined them in the moments before the crap hit the fan. This was hers. She had always loved fire. It was a destructive force, yes, but it was also beautiful. Her love for fire had started when she was only four years old and her foster parents had taken her camping. Her foster mother had been what many called a "prepper," believing it was best to know the skills you needed to survive and be ready for anything that came at you. Arte had been that particular foster mom's name. She had many foster mothers over the years before joining the Republic Infantry, but Arte was the one she remembered best. Arte had taught her a lot of things during their too-short years together, and a love and respect for fire had been one of them. Thanks to Arte, Wallace had known all about fire by the age of five. She knew how to start one, how to control one, and soon enough just how deadly fire could be.

She flicked the lighter closed a final time with a loud snap and tucked it back into her vest as the dropship lurched and left the bay of the *Hellbringer*, shooting out into space like a missile. Wallace imagined what the waves of dropships leaving the massive warship must look like, embers exploding from a disturbed campfire, springing away into the night sky. Almost instantly, which said a lot about the dropship's velocity, she felt the turbulence that came from it entering the atmosphere of Wycarri Prime. How beautiful the flames tearing over its hull must be, she thought. Their intensity, their rage, their brightness as they flared into being against the dropship's armored hull. The thought almost made her wish she was a pilot instead of a ground-pounder just so she could watch them through the dropship's forward window. Such a thing just wasn't in the cards for her though. The bulk of her education came from Arte's teachings, which she had taken to heart, and the public school system, which she had hated and had bored her to tears. The only classes she had ever done well in were the sciences like physics and chemistry, but even in them, she was no prize student. They were merely a means to an end, a path to widen and deepen her knowledge of fire and the universe as she saw it. Life and fire had much in common. They both burned bright only to wane and eventually be extinguished.

One day, Wallace hoped to leave the combat infantry behind and become a demolitions specialist. She had passed the tests time and time again with off-the-chart results, even if her answers were based more on intuition and natural talent than book knowledge. By all rights, she should have been able to be transferred into demolitions a year ago, but the data hacks who handled it all refused to approve it for her. "Psych reasons" was the answer she was always given when she questioned their decision. Apparently, they seemed to think she was as unstable as some of the explosives she would be working with if her transfer was granted. Her temperament was all wrong for that type of work, they told her. She was too flighty, too rash, and a thousand other excuses.

The bottom line was that they just didn't trust her and she knew it. As thus, all she could do was keeping going down the road she was on until either she got lucky or something changed.

The dropship was really shaking now as the violence of its atmospheric entry felt as if it was about to tear the ship apart. Loeb, beside her, lost his battle with the queasy he had to be feeling and threw up. His vomit splattered over him and what wasn't sprayed from his mouth outward to arc onto the floor ran along the front of his combat gear to drip onto it. The safety straps didn't allow one to bend any once they were in place and secured. Wallace shook her head at Loeb in disapproval but couldn't bring herself to feel bad for him. Rather, if she could have, she would've liked to punch him in the gut. The smell of the vomit was horrible. Wallace closed her eyes and tried to lose herself in the roughness of the ride to the surface of Wycarri Prime. Every jarring motion of the dropship's descent sent a trickle of anticipation running through her. With her eyes still closed, she reached over with her left hand, the tips of her fingers stroking the cold metal of the flame unit strapped to her right wrist. It wouldn't be long now until it was blisteringly hot and spewing blasts of searing flames at her enemies.

****

Captain Reggie Tanner clutched the arms of his command chair on the *Hellbringer*'s bridge. The massive ship, a hybrid carrier/battleship, had entered the Wycarri system and reached the planet without engagement just as planned. A few of the Mechi ships in the system managed to send missiles streaking through the Void her way, but her electronic counter-measures dealt with the bulk of them. The few that they hadn't met fire from the *Hellbringer*'s close-in defenses, ripping them to shreds before they could reach her. Not a single one had made contact with her shields. Captain Tanner knew he should be smiling ear to ear about that. It was rare that things played out according to plan. And he might have been had the *Hellbringer*'s sensor not picked up the Mechi fleet on the other side of Wycarri Prime. The bug fleet's engines were already active and full power. Even now, as his ship sat helplessly in orbit, deploying its ground forces, the bugs were burning those engines at maximum power to reach him. Their estimated time to intercept was less than three minutes. Just enough time to send the last of the dropships plunging into the planet's atmosphere and pull away from it. Not enough time to make his getaway without going head to head with them though.

"The last wave of dropships is away, Captain!" his XO, Thorson, shouted.

"Then what are we waiting for, Mr. Thorson?" he snapped. "Get us moving!"

"Yes, sir!" Thorson answered. Thorson knew how much trouble they would be in if the Mechi fleet was able to engage them too.

"We've cleared the planet's gravity well," Tanner's helmsman informed him.

Just as Captain Tanner was about to order him to engage the *Hellbringer*'s Void drive, his tactical officer screamed. "Missiles inbound, sir!"

The ships of the Mechi fleet had fired everything they had in their tubes at the *Hellbringer*. Captain Tanner glanced at the data read on the small screen of his chair arm to see that even the ship's computer was having trouble calculating just how many missiles that was.

"Evasive maneuvers! All power to shields!" he screamed, jerking forward and almost leaping from his command chair.

The ship's Electronic Counter-Measures and defense guns were already targeting the vast cloud of missiles blazing towards the *Hellbringer*. Mechi missiles disrupted by the ship's ECMs spun harmlessly away into the depths of the Wycarri system by the dozens. The explosions of detonating missiles lit up the emptiness of space between the *Hellbringer* and the bug fleet like a fireworks display flashing in a night sky. There were too many missiles to be stopped this time though. Captain Tanner jerked his eyes away from the bridge's forward view screen as the first of the missiles collided with the *Hellbringer*'s shields, engulfing them with fire. The shields held at fast, but the barrage of missiles was nowhere near its end.

"The shields are failing, sir!" Thorson screamed as the *Hellbringer* banked hard to port in an attempt to dodge at least some of the incoming fire.

Then the shields collapsed. The *Hellbringer*'s bridge shook as missile after missile hammered into its hull. A power surge ran through the bridge's systems as the comm. station erupted in a shower of sparks and flames that engulfed Ensign Buchanan. Her terrified cries of pain echoed across the bridge as she flung herself, her uniform and hair on fire, to the floor. Captain Tanner figured she was dead before her body ever made contact with it.

"Return fire!" Thorson was yelling at the top of his lungs as Captain Tanner glanced over at the XO.

The *Hellbringer*'s launchers spat missiles towards the approaching Mechi fleet. Captain Tanner didn't give a crap if they hit their targets or not. As tough and advanced as she was, not even the *Hellbringer* could fight an entire Mechi fleet alone. Getting out of the Wycarri system alive was all that mattered now.

"Void drive is prepped and ready, sir!" Nicholson shouted from where he sat at the helm controls.

"All hands, prepare for emergency Void jump," Captain Tanner barked over the ship's internal comm. and then glared at Nicholson. "For the love of all that's holy, punch it, man!"

Space around the massive carrier/battleship shimmered in the millisecond before it blinked out of existence, leaving the next waves of missiles blazing towards it and the Mechi fleet behind.

****

Dropship 8 slung itself hard to the right. The inertial pull of the movement made Shannon strain against his safety straps so they wouldn't cut into him. Despite his efforts, his face slapped into the thick part of the harness that came down from above him. He spat blood and ran his tongue over his front teeth to make sure they were all still there. They were. Shannon spat out a second mouthful of blood and looked around at the other soldiers near him. None of them, at least that he could see, had taken the sort of hit he had. Rage boiled inside him. He wanted to let loose a litany of curses but held his tongue. He was on thin ice with his C.O. as it was. Corporal Detato had almost had him thrown into the *Hellbringer*'s brig during the flight to the Wycarri system. Detato likely would have if time had permitted, but Shannon had been saved by the timing of the drop. Before Detato could do anything, action station klaxons had begun to blare throughout the ship. Shannon admitted to himself that he had lost it a little when Roberts had accused him of cheating in the last card game before the drop. The other members of Shannon's squad were always picking on him anyway. He was small, only about five feet six inches in height, and had the lean body of a runner, not the thickly muscle bound one that the other guys had. They all did weights, push-ups, and that junk while he usually had his nose buried in a comic book. Superheroes weren't cool when you were a grownup. Shannon still thought they were though. Back in his parents' mansion on the orbital city of New Carolina above Saturn, he had a collection that he had spent his entire life building. Real books too, not just the data files that most read on tablets these days. When he had joined up, his parents had continued to send him "trades" of his favorite series to wherever he was stationed. He was thankful for that because they kept him sane. Well, maybe not sane but at least together. Shannon had never planned on joining the Earth Republic Military. That had been forced on him by his father. His father, a former colonel, had pulled some strings and had Shannon drafted out of the college he was attending into the war with the Mechi. Shannon hated his old man for that just as he hated all the other soldiers around him now. They were all fools and idiots.

Growing up, Shannon had attended the best private schools that money could buy. His mother was a galaxy-wide known artist of renown. Her early art was already considered nearly priceless among collectors even though she was still alive and drawing. She did everything by hand just like the artists of the early comic books he so dearly loved. In fact, it was his mother who had given him his love for comics. She had taken him to an exhibit once that featured the works of long dead artists like Byrne, Perez, Kirby, and so many more. The characters and the world they depicted sucked him in like a moth to a flame. His mother had taken note of his interest and helped him buy his first real comic. After that, all his allowance and every other shred of money he could come across were saved up for such purchases. It made his mother proud that he appreciated art that way he did and even prouder when he announced to the family that he was going to pursue a career in writing. His father was the exact opposite. Being a military man from a long line of military men, his father demanded that Shannon grow up and perform his civic duty defending the Republic from the Mechi. Shannon wondered if his father cared if he even lived or died so long as the family name wasn't brought to shame by a son who opted for developing a gift for words over being a "man."

Glancing over at Roberts, he saw the man leering at him with the promise of vengeance to come. The red of warm blood seeped through the makeshift bandage Roberts had wrapped around his head to cover what remained of his left ear beneath his combat helmet. Shannon stifled a laugh. It was almost funny how the hardened, career soldier could get so upset over something as small as losing part of his ear in a fight that he started. Shannon liked to tell himself that he had only been defending himself against the bigger man when Roberts had yanked him out of his seat, threatening him. Roberts' hands had grabbed a hold of Shannon's shirt, crumbling it from the pressure of anger whitened, tight knuckles. As Roberts had let go with one hand to rear it back in order to take a swing at his face, Shannon had snaked free of Roberts' hold on him and went for blood. Lunging forward, into Roberts, he had taken both of them to the floor with him ending up on top. Knowing he didn't have the strength to fight Roberts fairly, Shannon had gone for Roberts' ear, his teeth closing on it and biting a large portion of it off. Roberts had thrown him off then, blood spurting from his wound, but Roberts' anger had taken on an edge of fear as the rest of the squad leaped in to pull the two of them apart.

Shannon didn't care what Roberts thought of him or about Roberts' threats. For all his muscle, Roberts was dumb and slow. Speeds and wits always won out at the end of the day. Shannon stuck out his tongue at Roberts in response to the man's leer. Roberts yelled something that Shannon couldn't make out over the howling of Dropship 8's straining engines. Whatever Roberts had said wasn't important anyway. Either of them could be dead within seconds of the dropship hitting the ground if not earlier. A single anti-aircraft missile could end the lives of everyone aboard the dropship before they even knew they were dead.

Corporal Detato was shouting something and gesturing at the dropship's rear door. Shannon figured it was time to go charging out into whatever hell awaited them on Wycarri Prime. The safety straps of his harness disengaged automatically and simultaneously with those of all of the other soldiers aboard Dropship 8. He watched Roberts go lunging forward in the wake of Corporal

Detato who was leading the charge towards the now blown-open rear door. Shannon held back, making sure he was near the last to go barreling towards it. Already, he could hear the screams of his fellow soldiers dying and enemy rounds pinging against the dropship's exterior armor through the open, rear door.

He made sure he wasn't the very last to move forward though. That would have looked odd, if anyone noticed in the chaos around him. With his rifle clutched tightly in his hands and ready, he gave a scream of his own and sprang forward to face whatever awaited him outside on the surface of Wycarri Prime.

****

"Come get some, you ugly mothers!" Brent "Metalface" Hyatt roared as he squeezed the trigger of his tri-barreled machine gun tight. Its barrels spun, humming as their ends thundered, spraying a stream of death into the Mechi on the street near where Dropship 11 had landed. Dropship 11 had touched down in the heart of the Mechi capital. The bugs hadn't yet been able to deploy a force to engage it. Nonetheless, the street was filled with panicked civilians and Brent was letting them have it full out. A bug was a bug was a bug. Rounds from his tri-barrel reduced what appeared to be a mother and several of her offspring to a blackish smear that covered the pavement. As Brent swept his machine ground around to his next set of targets, a Mechi that was dressed in what passed for a uniform among the bugs, who had at best two of the cybernetic enhancements that Mechi soldiers used as a part of his body, raised a handgun in Brent's direction. Brent snorted as the fire from his weapon tore the uniformed bug apart in an explosion of pulp and goo.

"Ease up, man!" his C.O., Williams, shouted at him over the thunder of Brent's weapon. No one else in the Butcher Dogs, their platoon, was firing like Brent was. Some of them were shooting but their targets were well chosen and not the random massacre that Brent was raining onto the Mechi in the street. "They're just civilians!"

Brent growled at Williams but took his finger off the trigger of his weapon and raised its barrels skyward. "If you say so, sir!" Brent snapped, the anger clear in his voice.

Williams was his commanding officer but that didn't mean Williams wasn't afraid of him. Everyone was afraid of old Metalface. On his first ever combat drop, some five years back, Brent had been too close to a grenade as it blew. The blast had ripped his face apart. The military docs had tried to convince Brent to allow them to graft him a new face grown from cloned flesh, but Brent refused. He also refused being booted out of the infantry due to his injury. His battalion's C.O. at the time, Colonel Spear, must have seen something in him because the colonel had gone to bat for Brent. In the end, Brent had consented to cybernetic replacements for the eye, most of his nose and mouth, and cheek that he had lost. Cybernetic argumentations were considered amoral, body defiling, and those who opted for them sick. Brent didn't see it like that. He liked the thought of them much more than "grown" tissue being made a part of him. If he was going to have parts of his body replaced in order to keep doing his job, then he dang well wanted replacement parts that were going to help him to that end. He didn't give a crap that he looked like a nightmarish Mechi/Human hybrid. All that mattered was that he could keep killing the damn bugs and killing a lot of them.

Brent's cybernetic eye glowed an eerie bright red as he glared at Williams. His C.O. took a step back.

"Just save your ammo for when the real Mechi show," Williams told him cautiously. "That's all I am saying, big guy."

Thinking over Williams' words for a moment, Brent was forced to admit there was wisdom in them, no matter how much he longed to start hosing the fleeing bugs in the street again.

The Mechi's military philosophy believed that the more cyber enhancements a soldier bore as a part of itself, the better a killing machine it would be. This, of course, only added to how scary any given Mechi soldier looked and served as an added psychological warfare bonus to the lethality of those cybernetics.

No two Mechi were alike. Not even as much as any two humans were alike in appearance. The Mechi were a strange, insect race of countless species all stemming from a single insectoid ancestor. One Mechi might have a body like a man's above the legs of a spider. Another might have wings and mandibles that covered its mouth. Some had hands, other pincers, and others still nothing at all but long, stabbing, spear-like arms that seemed to serve no other function than killing. Some had eyes like humans while others had a multitude of eyes clustered in two round orbs upon their faces. They all bled though, and they all could die. Brent liked that about the bugs. He liked how their exoskeletons sounded when they cracked and burst to pieces. He liked the softer flesh that some of the bugs had and how it looked as bullets ripped through it to emerge from the other side of their body. If any of the Mechi were small enough to crush under foot, he would have liked that sound too. Most Mechi were roughly human sized though, but a few far were larger. But again, they all bled, even if it was a blackish or sometimes yellowish pus, and that was enough to make Brent "Metalface" Hyatt smile from ear to ear.

He owed the bugs for what they had done to his family on Trevor II, and his sole purpose in life now was to make as many of the creatures as he could pay. Brent had only been a boy when the attack on Trevor II happened. It took place long before the formal war between the Mechi and the Earth Republic. Trevor II had been a thriving, outer-world colony of the Republic. The Mechi had raided Trevor II out of the blue, their ships suddenly appearing in orbit and dropping troops onto the planet. The colonists and the system's small defense fleet never stood a chance. Trevor II's militia died to the last man and woman attempting to save those they could. Their sacrifice was largely in vain. Of the thirty thousand colonists, only around five hundred survived the raid. Brent was headed home from school when the Mechi attack ships entered Trevor II's atmosphere and began blasting the town he lived in apart. He made it home only to find his parents dead. They had died trying to protect his brothers and younger sister. Brent would never forget the corpse of his father lying on the front steps of their house, shotgun in hand and scattered spent shell casings around his body. His father had been gutted by one of the Mechi and the long, purple snakes of his entrails leaked from his ruptured abdomen. His mother hung only a few feet from his father, speared to the house's outer wall next to its entrance. Of his brothers and younger sister, very little remained as the Mechi soldiers had taken the time to make a meal of them. The images of their gnawed-upon bones haunted him to this day. Brent knew he should have died with them. He should have been there by his father's side, gun in hand, defending his family. It didn't matter that he had only been nine at the time. Nine was old enough to hold a weapon and fight for what mattered in your life, and nothing had been more important to him than family. Now vengeance was all that filled his heart as nightmares of that day filled his sleep.

Thinking of it all caused him to lower his tri-barrel machine gun again, despite his C.O.'s orders. Killing a few more bugs could only ever be a good thing and he had plenty of ammo to spare. Brent took aim at another group of fleeing Mechi civilians and opened up on them, laughing, as the rounds from his weapon ripped through them and sent their dying bodies sprawling onto the street.

****

Enemy fire hammered the soldiers of Kurt's platoon. Dropship 13 had hit the ground just outside the Mechi capital's primary comm. center. And hit the ground was the only means to describe it. An anti-aircraft gun had clipped the dropship on its descent, sending it spiraling out of control. Kurt and a handful of others had survived the crash only to find themselves pinned down by the bugs. He and others were using the ruins of the ship as cover and returning fire as best they could. Thankfully, they weren't the only platoon assigned to deal with the comm. center. Dropship 14 had unleashed its cargo of the members of Hellhound platoon nearby, and those guys were pushing forward and gaining ground against the comm. center's defenders. If anything, the remnants of Kurt's own shattered platoon were helping them by serving as a distraction for them. The Mechi preferred their prey weak, and finishing off Kurt's platoon was too tempting of a target for the bugs to ignore.

Kurt wasn't an officer. He never had any intention of making the military his career. All he wanted to do was serve his time and get out. Today though, he had no choice but to step up and take over command as the platoon's C.O. and second were dead. The C.O. had died in the crash and his second had taken a round to his head that splintered his helmet, sending bits of his brain slashing over those closest to him when he was hit.

"Johnson, lay down some fire on the bugs on our right flank!" Kurt yelled. Johnson was the only surviving member of the platoon's heavy weapons squad. He was carrying a full out M-801. The huge weapon couldn't be fired from a standing position. It was too heavy for any single man to handle. That meant Johnson had to shift its position to take aim at the target Kurt had just given him. Kurt rushed to cover him as he did so. Kurt's rifle blazed on full-auto, spraying bullets at the closest of the Mechi soldiers. Several of them took hits but only a couple dropped from the wild stream of fire he sent their way. Kurt threw himself to the ground as they shot back at him. He heard their rounds whizzing through the air over him as the impact of his dive knocked the breath from his lungs. Gasping for air, he rolled over to come up into a firing position and squeezed his rifle's trigger again.

Nearby, he saw Lucas and Martin firing sporadically at the approaching Mechi troops. Lancaster's body lay between them behind the cover of a piece of the Dropship 13's broken hull. Lancaster had taken several hits to his chest, and his left shoulder was little more than a mess of mangled flesh. As he watched, Martin raised an RPG cannon onto his shoulder to take aim a cluster of bugs, but one of the Mechi pulled off a lucky shot that hit the cannon he held. Lucas, Martin, and Lancaster vanished in explosion that almost blinded Kurt and sent him bouncing along the ground from the shockwave of its blast.

Johnson had been able to bring his M-801 to bear on the charging Mechi though. The heavy machine gun's fire cut through the Mechi ranks like a scythe slashing through rows of corn. The innards of dozens of the cyber-enhanced bugs splattered from their thrashing bodies beneath its fire.

Kurt knew he and the other few survivors were fighting a losing battle. The way things were going, they would be overrun in the next few minutes, regardless of what they did. All his efforts to rally those left were pointless. They just didn't have the firepower or numbers to stop the bugs. He made a split-second decision to cut and run, whirling about and running full out away from the remains of Dropship 13. He didn't have a freaking clue where he was headed and no time to check the data that had been downloaded to the battalion's shared comm. link. Anywhere had to be better than where he was though. Kurt heard Johnson calling after him, but he ignored Johnson's panicked cries, his legs pumping under him as he ran. He had to get away. Dying today wasn't something he planned on doing, regardless of what it cost to make sure it didn't happen.

Back home on Wellhem IV, Diana was waiting on him. How he had ever ended up married to someone as beautiful as she was, he would never understand. Neither of them came from well-to-do families, and the war with the Mechi had crippled the Republic's industry base in the outer worlds. Joining up with the Republic military was what he had to do in order to make sure Diana was safe and that the child they hoped to have someday would be provided for. Wellhem IV was one of the few outer worlds that the war with the Mechi had driven into utter chaos. It was a fringe colony, close to the frontlines. That combined with the damage done to its economy from the war had left its population turning on itself to survive. His joining up made sure that Diana was given a home at the Republic defense base on Wellhem IV, the safest place left on the planet. He missed her so much, every passing second. He longed to feel her arms about him and often dreamed of the curves of her body pressed up against his own flesh. Before he had shipped out, Kurt promised her he would make it home, alive and in one piece, and that promise mattered more to him than his duty ever would when push came to shove.

By the grace of God, he made it clear of the killzone that the site of Dropship 13's crash had become. He ducked behind the cover of a tree, looking back at it. The Mechi had pressed their way inside the perimeter of fire he had the other survivors set up. The battle was truly up close and personal for those left alive there now, not that there were that many who had yet to die. Guilt clawed at him, but he shook himself and reminded himself that it wasn't his job to keep those he was watching die alive. That job had belonged to his C.O., not him.

Kurt knelt behind the tree, keeping as still as he could so as to not attract the attention of any Mechi might happen to glance in his direction and started wondering what in the devil he was going to do now.

****

Krellman's pistol cracked as it spat a round, point blank, into the hissing mouth of a Mechi female. Her brains exited the backside of her head in a spray of black blood, chitin, and brain matter. Krellman stepped around her corpse as it fell to bounce down the steps of the stairwell. He was moving fast, but everything seemed to be in slow motion to his heightened senses. Gunter was following close to him. The big guy was having a difficult time keeping up with him, but Krellman knew they couldn't slow down. They had to reach the top of the building as quickly as possible. Grinder platoon was counting on them. He could hear the fighting in the streets outside the building. Things were really heating up out there. When the dropships assigned to the city landed, there had been very little resistance from the Mechi as they had caught the bugs utterly by surprise. Now though, the first organized units of actual Mechi troops were beginning to reach them. Grinder platoon was still managing to hold its position, but Krellman had heard over the battalion's shared comm. net that several platoons were already lost. He knew Dropships 13 and 18 had crashed and everyone aboard 13 was presumed K.I.A. Krellman had known some of the guys on 13. He felt a pang of loss as their faces played through his mind even as he continued to sprint up the stairs towards the building's roof.

Reaching the door that led onto the roof, Krellman tried to kick it open and failed. His combat boot thudded into it but only shook it on its hinges. Cursing at his failure, he stepped aside as Gunter came charging up towards the door. The big grunt aimed his shoulder at it as he ran. Gunter crashed into the door at a full out and continued on through it as its wood gave way to the sheer juggernaut of force that he was.

"You coming?" Krellman heard Gunter call to him from outside and laughed.

Krellman darted onto the roof and instantly looked around, picking his spot. He found a good one that overlooked a three-way angle of the streets below and slid his pistol into the holster on his hip. He shrugged his custom-modified rifle from his shoulders into his hands and began to check it. As he did so, he tapped the comm. activator on his helmet. "This is Bravo One. I'm in position. Start calling 'em out!"

Behind him, Gunter took up a position guarding the door they had come through. It was unlikely that any Mechi troopers would be storming through, at least for a bit, but Gunter wasn't known for taking chances. He did his job by the book. This was their fourth drop together, and Krellman was glad to have the big guy as his support and spotter again. Every sniper needed a trustworthy mate watching their back when the crap hit the fan as hard and fast as it was on this drop.

Multiple voices were crying out to him over his helmet's comm., all calling for fire support. Various corporals and other squad C.O.s were demanding he take out some of the Mechi near their positions. Krellman listened to them, prioritizing them as best he could in his head. He leaned against the edge of the roof and sprang into action. His first target was a group of Mechi approaching a squad of soldiers from an alleyway on their flank. No one had called them in as one of his targets and that was why he picked them. Likely, no one, not even the squad they were closing in, knew they were there. He took careful aim, released the air in his lungs in something resembling a long sigh, and got to work.

His first shot blew apart the skull of one of the Mechi. The other bugs around it panicked. There was chaos in the alley as his second shot severed the spine of another member of the small group and the rest dove for cover. One of the Mechi fired wildly at the windows above the alley. The rounds from the bug's weapon shattered the glass of the windows there in an attempt to take out the sniper that was obviously killing its comrades. Krellman smirked at the bugs' helplessness as he watched for them a second longer through his scope. He could see that the sound of the gunfire tipped off the squad of soldiers to the bugs' location. His job was with this particular target was done.

Krellman shifted his position slightly as he took aim at his next target. A bug personnel carrier was roaring its way along the main street. A bug, its upper body sticking out of its roof, was laying down heavy fire with the vehicle's top-mounted machine gun. Krellman didn't bother with the gunner. He went straight for the carrier's driver. The carrier's forward window was tougher than he thought. It took two shots to get the job done, but with his second shot, its glass sprayed inward over the driver even as that bullet plunged into the driver's chest. The carrier jerked to the right, then to the left, before its wheels struck a mound of debris in the road. The bump tipped it over onto its side, skidding along the road in a shower of sparks before it finally exploded into a blossoming ball of fire and bits of flying shrapnel.

Allowing himself a smile, Krellman took aim at a Mechi, well behind the main lines of the battle, who was in the process of lifting something akin to an RPG to its shoulder. He targeted the weapon the bug held, not the bug. His bullet slammed into the weapon, detonating whatever ordnance was within it. The bug and those closest to it died instantly as its blast cooked them alive.

"We got company coming!" Gunter shouted at him, gesturing towards the door he was guarding.

"Frag it," Krellman muttered. He had just been getting into a groove. Lifting his rifle, he rushed to Gunter's side. "Any idea how many?"

"Too many." Gunter frowned as he pulled a grenade from his belt.

Krellman met his eyes and nodded.

Gunter armed the grenade and tossed it through the door into the stairwell below.

Krellman and Gunter leaped for cover as the grenade's blast shook the roof as chunks of broken and flaming debris erupted from the doorway. The next thing Krellman knew, Gunter was yanking him to his feet.

"Come on, man! We gotta move!" Gunter yelled at him.

Krellman barely heard the words. His ears were ringing as he shook Gunter's hand from him. "This way," he ordered, running towards the far side of the roof. As he had looked around for a place to set up, Krellman had noticed a smaller building to the right of the one they were on. Gunter followed after him as Krellman picked up his pace to a full-out sprint and flung himself over the edge of the roof. He hit the roof of the shorter building, rolling, with a grunt of pain. Gunter landed next to him with a loud thud.

"You're gonna get us killed pulling crap like this one day," Gunter laughed, happy that they both had made it and were still alive.

Krellman ignored Gunter's comment as he got to his feet. He raised his rifle and blew apart the locking mechanism on the door that had to lead into the building they had just leaped onto. Mechi troops were already beginning to reach the edge of the roof they had left. Krellman reached the door just as they opened fire. Gunter was running towards him, zigging and zagging as he came in an attempt to dodge the bullets that were peppering the rooftop around him.

Jerking up his rifle, Krellman returned fire as Gunter caught up to him. He let Gunter go by him into the building first and then dove through the doorway. The interior of the building was dark. Its power must have been knocked out by the fighting in the street outside. Krellman flipped down his helmet's visor to look at the stairwell below them in infrared. There was no sign of Mechi troops on the stairs.

"After you." He grinned at Gunter.

Gunter grunted but didn't argue with him. The big man led the way down the stairs.

****

Brent "Metalface" Hyatt hunkered down behind a mass of debris in the street. Williams lay twitching on the ground next to him. When the Mechi had gotten their act together, they had hit the platoons deployed in the capital hard and fast. They had been able to mobilize much faster than anyone had anticipated they could, and their numbers seemed endless. For every bug Brent killed, it seemed like four more took its place. He glanced over at where Williams lay. His C.O. was as good as dead even if a medic could get to him. The burst of Mechi fire that hit him had punched holes through his combat armor that caved its metal inward into his chest. Each breath he took sounded like a wheezing scream. The street around Williams was smeared with the bright red of his blood. The fact that Williams was even still conscious showed what a tough S.O.B. he was. Brent didn't waste time lying to Williams that it was all going to be okay. Williams reached out a hand towards him but Brent ignored it, refocusing his attention on the Mechi troops in the street up ahead of their position. He popped up over the top of the debris he was using as cover long enough to send a spray of bullets blazing from his tri-barrel in their direction. He was rewarded with the sound of several Mechi squealing in pain as he ducked back down. The rest of the platoon wasn't faring any better. Over half of them or more, Brent guessed, were dead based on the number of human bodies scattered about that he could see from where he was. Any chance of pressing onward into the city was as dead as Williams was about to be.

Panicking voices flooded the battalion's comm. net and not just from the capital. The Mechi were hitting back harder than expected everywhere. Someone in intelligence had screwed up big time in gauging the bug's response time to this op. It was time to cut and run as far as Brent was concerned. He needed a distraction though. Something to keep the bugs from fire directed anywhere but at him as he made a break for it or at least something to force them to take cover for a moment.

The door to the building on his left burst open and two figures came running out of it. Brent whirled towards them almost cutting them to pieces with his tri-barrel. Thankfully, he caught himself at the last moment before he squeezed the weapon's trigger. The two figures wore colonial combat gear.

"Over here!" Brent shouted at them.

They joined him behind the cover of the debris. Brent saw the rifle one of them was carrying and knew the man had to be a sniper. The other guy was likely his support and was almost as big as he was himself.

"Thanks!" the sniper told him. "Thought we were screwed there for sure."

The sniper didn't seem phased at all by the sight of Brent's face. The other man though stared at him, eyes wide, in shock. "You're the guy they call Metalface!" he rasped and then managed to bring his voice down to more normal tone. "Hyatt, right?"

Brent nodded.

"I'm Gunter and my little buddy there is Krellman," the man almost as big as he was told him.

Mechi bullets continued to pound against the pile of debris.

"Is it really this bad everywhere?" Brent asked.

"It ain't good," Krellman answered. "We had barely gotten set up and going before the bugs drove us out of position."

"Either of you guys carrying a grenade?" Brent snapped.

"Got one in my pack," Gunter answered.

"Then use it, man," Brent snarled. "If we don't get out of here, we're dead men. Another bug APC could come rolling through here at any moment."

Gunter hurled the grenade over the top of the mound of the debris and all three of them took off running as it detonated.

Brent's long legs put him ahead of Gunter and Krellman, but they caught up to him quickly. The three of them darted into an alleyway several yards from where they had been pinned down. Brent kept the lead as they sprinted through it. When they reached its other side and burst onto a street again, Krellman shouted, "The dropships are this way!" and picked up his pace, passing Brent as they ran.

****

Kurt didn't have a clue how long he had been sitting amid the trees at the edge of the city. He had watched all the other members of his platoon who survived Dropship 13's crash die at the hands of the Mechi troops that had overrun them. The Mechi had moved about through their corpses, cutting trophies from their bodies and eating bits of them as time permitted. The Mechi hadn't tarried long though. The fighting over in the area where Dropship 14's soldiers had charged the comm. center had grown more intense with every passing minute. It seemed to go on forever before it finally started to die out. The only clue he had as to which side had gotten the upper hand in the battle was that the Mechi comm. center hadn't been blown like it was supposed to have been. That was a very bad sign. If the platoon from Dropship 14 had been driven back though, they hadn't retreated in his direction or he would have seen them.

It began to sink in that he was really and truly alone. No one would be coming to save him. If he wanted to live, he was going to have to get up off his butt and get moving. His only hope was to reach one of the dropships before they were all pulled out. If what he had seen here at the comm. center was any indication, the entire op. had fallen apart. The battalion had lost the initiative and was likely fighting for its life against an entire city of Mechi intent on making it pay for the damage it had been able to do.

Kurt's throat burned from all the smoke in the air. He dug a bottle of water from his pack and chugged half of it before twisting its top back on. As he put the bottle into his pack again, he looked around, trying to decide on the safest route to where the closest dropship might be. After a moment, he had to admit to himself that he didn't have a clue where he was, much less where one of the battalion's dropships might be. Wycarri Prime's sun was beginning to sink in the sky. It would be dark soon. Whether he knew where he was going or not, moving out now would be a lot smarter than waiting and being forced to try to find his way around in the dark on an alien planet.

He hadn't tried using his helmet's comm. because he didn't want to be forced to explain how he was alive when the rest of Dropship 13's platoon wasn't. Kurt knew he wasn't a good liar. No matter what kind of reasonable story he told, and in this kind of F.U.B.A.R-ed mess, there were plenty he could run with, he knew he would flub it up if he was pressed on it. Getting charged with deserting would be just as bad as having a Mechi bullet leaving him gutted and dying in the dirt of these woods. Either way, he would never see Diana again. Not knowing where he was though, he had no choice but to try his comm. and call for help. He tapped the side of his helmet activate it, his hand trembling as he did so, only to find that it didn't work. Jerking his helmet off, he looked at it and saw that a Mechi round had grazed its side. He hadn't felt the bullet as it hit. He must have been too pumped up on fear and adrenaline to feel it as he had run. Nonetheless, the bullet had damaged his helmet's comm., leaving it inoperable. He didn't have the training to fix it. Trying would be just a waste of time.

Putting his helmet back on, Kurt changed out the magazine in his rifle, making sure he had a fresh one ready to go if the Mechi found him or he stumbled onto them as he moved out. Picking a direction that he hoped was south, which was where the dropships were supposed to be, he started through the trees at a cautious pace. As much as time was against him, running headlong through the woods was a bad idea. There had been no sign that the Mechi were anywhere nearby for some time now, but that didn't mean they weren't. The bugs could be very clever when they needed to be and one of them could very well be waiting in ambush out there somewhere.

Kurt's thoughts drifted homeward again as he walked. He thought about Wellhem IV and hoped Diana was okay there. Odds were that she was. Still, when he got home, he planned on using the money from his tour to give them a new life and leave the unrest and poverty of Wellhem IV behind them. They wouldn't have enough money to resettle on Earth like they had always dreamed of doing, but they surely would have enough to move to a more inner world of the Republic like Mars if they were willing to gamble on finding good work when they got there. And Diana might just be able to do that. She had a degree in teaching, and Mars was a thriving world with a huge population. Surely, there would be a school somewhere on the planet that needed a teacher. As to him, well, Mars was a mining world. If it came to it, he could find work as a miner until something better came along. Mining was rough and dangerous work, but he knew he could do it if he had Diana to come home to at night.

A memory of how her hair smelled hit him and stopped in his tracks, relishing it. Something moving in the trees ahead of him though snapped his attention to the woods surrounding him. He ducked where he stood, dropping into a squatting, combat stance. In the distance, he could hear the clicking and chattering noises of at least two Mechi voices conversing. Sinking even closer to the ground, he crawled, rifle in hand, into a patch of brush, keeping his movements as quiet as he could. Where there were two of the bugs, there were likely more. Figuring that keeping out of sight and hoping the bugs didn't notice him was his best option, Kurt stayed in the brush, barely daring to even breathe. He told himself that it wasn't that he was a coward, it was that he had too much to live for.

The chattering voices of the two Mechi drew closer. He had no idea what they were saying to each other, but they still sounded calm by bug standards, maybe even bored. They came into view, wandering into the small clearing he had crawled out of to seek cover. Both of the bugs were covered in the cyber-enhancements that Mechi soldiers usually had. One of the two was more metal than exoskeleton. Its mechanical eyes burned a hot yellow in the growing twilight. The other bug had legs like a spider below its body. The metal armor grafted onto them gleamed in the little light that there was. Its two arms rounded out the number of limbs attached to its body making it truly an even eight. Its eyes were massive, bulbous shapes that protruded from its face. Thick mandibles covered its slit of a mouth. Both of the bugs carried standard-issue Mechi rifles. Kurt saw that the less armored one would be an easy kill. A shot to its head from behind would end it. If it had been alone, Kurt would have taken the shot and been done with it. The fully cybered-up Mechi though stayed his hand and assured him that taking cover had been the best thing to do. That bug looked like one anyone in their right mind would think twice before taking it on.

Seconds ticked by like hours as Kurt waited for the two Mechi to pass on through the small clearing and vanish out of sight. When they finally did, he waited another full five minutes before leaving the cover of the brush and scrambling to his feet. There had been no other sign of Mechi following behind them. His best guess was that the two of them were a patrol and out here alone. Kurt resumed heading south towards where he hoped the battalion's dropships were still waiting.

****

The attack on Wycarri Prime's spaceport had been stopped in its tracks from the moment it started. The powers that be had expected it to be a difficult target and heavily guarded but no one had imagined that one of the ships docked at it would be carrying several mech squads on their way off-world to the frontlines of the war.

Mechi mechs were huge and horrid things. They stood between twelve and eighteen feet tall, all armor and weapons. The mechs emerged, bounding from the transport they were aboard, to engage the Republic infantry trying to encircle the spaceport and cut it off from any help that might come to aid it from the capital. The Republic soldiers died by the dozens as the heavy mechs opened up on them. Some mechs equipped with anti-personnel machine guns rained fire onto them before they ever got into the positions the op. plans had assigned to them. Wallace watched one soldier ahead of her take so many hits that it looked like his body actually exploded beneath the barrage of bullets that tore into him. She flung herself to the ground, playing dead with his blood staining her combat gear. From where she lay, she listened to the screams of the men and women of the platoon assigned to take out the spaceport as they were decimated by the mechs. When the mech had turned its attention elsewhere, Wallace hurled herself to her feet and ran. As the mechs continued their systemic slaughter of the Republic soldiers who had accompanied her to the spaceport, she ducked beneath the cover of a Mechi freighter. Wallace's squad was dead. She was its only survivor. And she wanted vengeance.

Wallace knew she couldn't change the tide of the battle or take the spaceport out by herself, but she sure as hellfire could give the Mechi some payback. One of the mechs came lumbering by the freighter she crouched under. She waited until it was basically on top of her and then sprang from beneath the freighter into its path. The mech pilot had no time to react as she raised her flame unit up to its driver's compartment. Most bug mech had open driver compartments, as they believed the cybernetic armor grafted onto them was enough protection. At this kind of range, for a weapon like the flame unit Wallace carried, it wasn't. The stream of fire from the unit on her arm blasted the mech's pilot melting the bug where it sat inside the middle of the mech's torso. The bug pilot thrashed about as its exoskeleton melted and its eyes burst, like cooking popcorn, and turning into patches of boiling goo. The mech stopped dead in its tracks, smoke rolling up towards the sky as its pilot and control systems burned.

Another mech was quickly approaching her from her right. Wallace could almost feel its targeting systems trying to lock onto her as she dived back beneath the freighter and continued on under it to emerge on its other side. She heard the whooshing sound of missiles leaving the mech's shoulder mounted launchers as she ran. The freighter behind her erupted into an explosion of flames and debris as the missiles struck it. The blast picked her up like a ragdoll and flung her forward, adding to her own momentum. Wallace slammed into the ground with a grunt as the breath was knocked from her lungs. Gasping for air, she forced herself to her feet and kept on running.

The panicked screams and chatter coming over the battalion's comm. net told her that the attack on the spaceport wasn't the only part of the operation that was falling apart. From the sound of things, the entire battalion had been forced into retreat. That meant everyone who was still alive would be heading for the closest landing zones in regards to the target they had been assigned.

The bulk of the Republic dropships were to the south at the battalion's primary rally point for extraction, and that was where she headed. A mech came bounding into her path. It was one of the smaller mechs, designed for speed and to take out infantry. Both of its arms ended in tri-barreled machine guns. They came up at her as she raised her own weapon. Wallace managed to fire first. A great blast of fire from the unit on her wrist washed over the front of the mech. Unlike the larger, lumbering one she had just killed, this one had a sealed pilot's compartment. Its optic and other exterior sensors melted under the fury of the fire being sprayed over it, but otherwise, it was too tough for her flame unit to do any real damage without it taking a prolonged blast. Wallace didn't have time to keep her flames trained onto it, not when the tri-barrels of its machine guns began to spin and spat fifty rounds a second in her direction. She would have died right then and there had not another Republic soldier come charging out of nowhere to tackle her. The two of them went rolling through the dirt out of the mech's line of fire.

As the man who had tackled her rose and yanked her to her feet, she realized with a start that it Sergeant Major Wilson himself, second-in-command of the entire battalion. Her eyes bugged out as she stared at him. Wilson spun to face the mech that was adjusting its aim to target them. He carried a weapon that looked like a cross between a shotgun and an RPG launcher. When he fired it, the recoil was enough to make him grunt in pain. A quartet of mini-rockets flew from the weapon's square set of four barrels into the mech. Their impact and the explosion that followed picked the mech up from the ground, knocking it backwards, its entire front reduced to nothing more than jagged and burning metal when it finally thudded to the ground, lying on its back.

The sergeant major was already pumping the loading mechanism on the underside of his weapon to reload its four barrels as another mech came charging towards them. It was another of smaller anti-infantry ones.

Wilson gave her a shove. "Run, trooper! I got this!"

Wallace didn't need to be told twice. She pushed her body to its limits, pouring on all the speed she could muster. Behind her, she heard Wilson's weapon thunder again. Glancing over her shoulder without slowing down, she saw that the sergeant major had missed his target this time. The mech had managed to hurl itself to the right just in time. The quartet of mini-rockets streaked by its side through the spot it had been in half a second before to impact with against the side of a docked Mechi warship. They exploded there, doing little to huge ship's armored hull. Sergeant Major Wilson didn't have time to reload. The mech's tri-barrels spun, blazing away at him. Wilson tried to turn to and run for cover but the bullets hammered into his back, tearing through combat armor and flesh alike. His chest exploded outwards, flinging bits of the bones of his ribs and pieces of his organs forward in front of him.

Clearing the edge of the spaceport, Wallace headed across the open field towards the woods surrounding it. A mass of trees, up ahead in the direction she was running, exploded as a cluster of missiles fired from a mech's shoulder launcher blew them apart. Wallace zagged, changing her course slightly, as she kept up her speed. The muscles of her legs burned despite the adrenaline pumping through her. She didn't look back. Doing so would only slow her down. Either she would make it to the cover of the trees or she wouldn't. It all came down to how lucky she was now and she knew it.

****

Kurt paused at the edge of the clearing in the woods. His pace had been a hurried one but also cautious in its nature. He kept to the cover of the trees as he peered into the clearing. A battle had taken place here. There were bodies, both human and Mechi, scattered everywhere. Amid them, a thin man dressed in Republic combat gear was moving from body to body, squatting beside each for a moment before moving on to the next. Kurt didn't have a freaking clue what the guy was doing. Something about the situation seemed utterly wrong to him. Still, the guy was a human and part of the battalion, so Kurt was happy to see someone else alive.

"Hey!" Kurt called out as he stepped from the trees, rifle aimed in the guy's direction. The man dropped something he had taken from the body he was squatting next to hurriedly and rose to his feet, wiping his hands on his pants. They left smears of red on the cloth where he rubbed them.

"This was supposed to be an extraction point," the pale, thin trooper told him. "The bugs got here before we did, I guess."

Kurt nodded, walking closer to the man, his rifle still at the ready. "Yeah, I can see that," Kurt answered. "I'm Kurt."

"Specialist Shannon Watkins," the man replied. "You alone?"

Kurt nodded again. "I was on Dropship 13 went it crashed. Barely made it out alive."

Shannon's question was perfectly normal for the situation. Any trooper would want to know if help had just shown up to save the freaking day for them. Shannon hadn't asked it like that though. Something about the tone of his voice seemed to the question an entirely different feel and not one that put Kurt at ease.

Kurt pointed at the body Shannon had been squatting over. "You gathering up ammo or something?"

Shannon shook his head. "No. I was … just checking to make sure they were all really dead."

Kurt didn't know what to say to that response. Thankfully, Shannon didn't give him a chance to reply.

"I can't tell you how glad I am to see someone else left alive." Shannon smiled. It was a cold and hollow mockery of a real smile that sent shivers running along Kurt's spine. "I thought I might be the only one who was still breathing that wasn't already back at the main extraction zone."

"The comm. on my helmet took a hit," Kurt said, almost wishing he hadn't just blurted out that information. "Yours working?"

"Fully functional." Shannon beamed at him. "That's how I know where everyone else is. They're all trying to get off this planet in a hurry. I don't think it's going to happen though."

"What? Why?" Kurt asked.

"I was able to modify my comm. a bit while I've been poking about here," Shannon said. "I tuned it to pick up the general band the Mechi are using. From what I've been able to glean from listening to the bugs, they've been able to scramble a good number of fighters despite the attack on the spaceport. The dropships will be like sitting ducks for them. Even if the dropships make it into the air before the fighters reach them, well ... I hate to say it, but we're likely lucky to be stuck out here."

"You can understand Mechi?" Kurt asked, stunned.

"Bits and pieces, yeah," Shannon told him. "Enough to know that the dropships won't be reaching orbit anyway."

Kurt's legs went weak under him. He barely managed to stay on his feet from the shock of the news Shannon shared with him. Only then did he notice that Shannon wasn't carrying a rifle like he was. Shannon held a knife in his right hand. Its blade dripped blood and not all of it the black crap that pulsed through the veins of the bugs.

Shannon came at him so fast Kurt didn't even have time to squeeze his rifle's trigger. The thin man ripped his rifle from his grasp and gave him a shove that sent Kurt toppling into the dirt. Kurt landed on his butt, staring up at Shannon as the little man turned the rifle he had stolen around to level its barrel at Kurt's forehead.

"Who in the devil are you?" Kurt shouted up at him.

The question seemed to confuse Shannon. "I'm Specialist Shannon Watkins," he said again. "Didn't I tell you that already, Kurt? You weren't listening, were you? That's rude, you know?"

Kurt swallowed hard, staring into the barrel of his own rifle, and chose his next words very carefully. "Look, Shannon ..." he said, "we're both on the same side. The bugs are the enemy, and they're going eat us both if we give them the chance. We need to be working together if either one of us ever wants to make it home."

"Who said I wanted to go home?" Shannon asked. "I was rather having a good bit of fun before you came along and interrupted it."

Kurt glanced around, noticing that the mutilation of the bodies in the clearing went far beyond the wounds that had killed them. One of the human bodies was stripped naked and cut open from its groin to the bottom of its throat. Kurt tried to hide the horror and disgust he felt, but it was no use. He leaned over sideways, vomiting in the grass.

Shannon cackled loudly. "You have a weak stomach for a soldier. If you're wondering, that guy was my C.O. Real wanker of one. His name was Roberts. Threatened to lock me up because I was cheating at cards and taught the cheater a lesson I figured he would remember for the rest of his life. It's sad that it was so short."

Kurt wiped his mouth with the backside of his hand and looked at Roberts' corpse again.

"I think I tossed his tongue somewhere over that way." Shannon gestured across the sea of bodies littering the clearing. "I mean, if you want to see it too."

"I'm good," Kurt said. "Look, Shannon, it doesn't matter what you've done. For all I care, you can kill as many folks as you like. I just want to get home. Neither one of us is doing that unless we work together."

Shannon stared at him. "You … You don't care what I've done?"

Kurt shook his head. "I just want to go home. That's all. And I need your help to do it."

Slinging Kurt's rifle onto his shoulder by its strap, Kurt leaned forward to offer him a hand up.

"Okay, Kurt, let's say I believe you," Shannon said as Kurt took his hand and was pulled up to his feet. "What's to keep you from turning me in for this when we do get home?"

"You have my word that I won't," Kurt answered, meeting Shannon's eyes. It was like looking into pools of swirling chaos. Shannon was utterly insane.

"Don't know why, but I really think you're being honest with me, Kurt." Shannon grinned, his lips parting like those of a feral cat. "Tell you what, I'll help you get home. *My* word on that. But I'll be keeping this rifle of yours for the time being. It has a good feel to it. You can grab one from them if you like." Shannon nodded at the dead surrounding them.

Kurt looked around, trying not to step on any of the dead, as he searched for a weapon that worked for him. He found an automatic shotgun in the hands of a woman with her guts spilling out of her and wrested it from her dead hands. Shannon nodded at him as if approving of his choice.

"Off we go then, buddy." The psychopath laughed. "You take point. I'll be right behind you … all the way home."

After checking his new shotgun to make sure its magazine was fully loaded, Kurt sighed as he led Shannon into the woods, and the two of them headed south.

****

Four dropships were lost, one to a crash, two to enemy fire while inbound, and a fourth had reported reaching its position, but after that, all contact with it had been lost. Dropship Alpha was larger than any of the other dropships due to the added command center aboard it between its pilot and rear compartment. Lieutenant Colonel Lyle stood in the command center, his gaze roaming from one tactical display screen to another. His support staff shared the small room with him. Hector, his personal tech, and Samantha, his comm. Officer, worked frantically at their stations as his aide, Sym, stood at his side. Things had seemed to be going well at first, but the tide of the battle on Wycarri Prime had shifted very quickly and not in favor of his battalion. The Mechi were much more ready for an assault than anyone expected.

Lyle had ordered all the dropships and their defenders to regroup just south of the Mechi capital at the prearranged rally point established for the battalion. All he could do now was try to hold on and wait. Lyle didn't believe in leaving anyone behind if it could be helped. Time was running out though. Hector had informed him that the Mechi had launched several squadrons of fighters and that those fighters were in route to the dropships' position. If they reached it before the dropships were in the air, it was the end for them all. The dropships were tough and designed to take heavy fire, but they lacked real weapons when it came to air-to-air combat. They were also slow and cumbersome ships in comparison to any type of fighter craft. If the Mechi fighters in route engaged them, it would be a massacre. Lyle wanted to pace, but there was no room for it in the small command center of dropship Alpha, so he rubbed at the stubble on his cheeks with the fingers of his right hand instead.

"Estimated time of arrival on those fighters?" Lyle asked.

"Less than two minutes, sir," Hector answered him.

Lyle's hand rose higher as he ran his fingers through his hair. "And how many troopers out there are still on their way here?"

Sym shook his head. "There's no means of knowing that, sir. At least two-thirds of the battalion's strength remains unaccounted for. A good portion of that number are likely dead, but as I said, we can't be sure. The Mechi had attacked much faster and harder than we thought they could."

Lyle restrained himself, biting his lip so that he didn't snap at Sym. The pressure was getting to him and he knew it.

Spinning around in his seat to look up at him, Hector said, "We need to go if we're going, Colonel."

The fighting around the dropships was intense. The Mechi was pressing hard to destroy them where they sat despite the fighters in route to deal with them. It was taking everything his men had just to hold the ground they were on, and the causality list continued to grow with each passing minute.

Finally, Lyle nodded. "Okay. Order the men to disengage and board the dropships. I want all our dropships here airborne as soon as possible."

"Yes, sir!" Hector barked. "I'll spread the word."

Lyle heard Dropship Alpha's rear door clang up into place. Within seconds, her engines roared, and he felt the dropship lift off. He could see the other dropships following after her on the command center's tactical screens.

"Any word on from the *Hellbringer*?" Lyle asked.

"None, Colonel," Samantha reported. "I'm still broadcasting our emergency extraction code on all Republic frequencies."

"That's not good," Sym commented.

Lyle knew what he meant. If the dropships reached orbit and the *Hellbringer* wasn't there to meet them, they would be even worse off there than they were here. The Mechi's fighters were deadly, but the cruisers and battleships that had surely assembled around the planet after the *Hellbringer*'s run on it were worse. Against them, the dropships stood no chance whatsoever. They'd be blown to bits by the first wave of missiles those ships launched.

"Keep trying to reach Captain Tanner and the *Hellbringer*," Lyle ordered Samantha.

"All dropships are airborne," Hector reported.

The Mechi forces on the ground refused to give up the battle even as the Republic dropships took flight. Lieutenant Colonel

Lyle watched as Dropship 9 was struck by a surface-to-air missile and died in a flash of heat and light that lit the night sky.

"Mechi fighters inbound!" Hector shouted.

The first squadron of Mechi fighters came howling through the air towards the dropships. Their forward cannons blazed as they drew closer. Dropship Alpha shuddered as enemy fire slammed into its armor hull. Lyle knew that as soon as the dropships broke out of Wycarri Prime's atmosphere, the bugs' fighters would no longer be able to target them.

"More power to the engines," Lyle screamed over the command center's comm. to Dropship Alpha's pilots.

"We're already at maximum," Jim, Dropship Alpha's co-pilot, answered him.

Dropship Alpha was shaking badly, almost as if she was on the verge of tearing herself apart. Fire from the next wave of Mechi fighters plunging through the dropships' ranks hammered her. This time, the rounds from the fighters must have hit something vital. The lights in the small command center went out, and Dropship Alpha lurched. The last images Lyle saw on the tactical screens before they went dark showed dropship after dropship exploding in the night sky. Lieutenant Colonel Lyle and his aide, Sym, were tossed about the small command center, bouncing against its walls, as Dropship Alpha went into a spin and dropped sharply, her nose now pointed back towards the surface of Wycarri Prime.

"We're going down!" Hector shouted from where he sat strapped in at the command center's sensor station. "Hold on!"

Lyle managed to grab the edge of Samantha's comm. station. She reached out, taking hold of him and clung to him tightly. Sym wasn't so lucky. He was slammed up into the command center's ceiling with such force that Lyle heard the cracking sound of breaking bones. When Sym's body toppled downwards again, his neck tilted at an unnatural angle on his shoulders and the white of bone protruded from his bent and broken left arm.

As Sym's body continued to flop about Dropship Alpha's command center, Lyle, with Samantha's help, pulled himself into a seat and fought to strap himself in. With the power out and the dropship's internal comm. knocked offline, there was no word from the pilot compartment on the ship's status. Lyle didn't need to hear from the pilots to know that the ground was coming up fast though. He snapped the last of the straps of his safety harness in place and began to mumble a prayer just as Dropship Alpha crashed into the surface of Wycarri Prime.

****

Wallace didn't know if any others from the platoons assigned to take out Wycarri Prime's spaceport had survived or not. Alone, she stumbled through the dark woods, heading south, while knowing she would likely never reach the rally point in time. Still, she had to try though.

Since she had escaped the battle at the spaceport, there had been no signs of the Mechi pursuing her. Eventually, they would come for her, but for now, the Mechi forces were busy dealing with much larger things than a single soldier on foot. She had run for so long that her body was on the verge of collapse. It took everything she had just to keep walking. Putting one foot in front of the other was a sheer act of will at this point, but she knew she needed to keep going. Not just to try to reach the dropships but to put as much distance between herself and whatever Mechi forces were behind her at the spaceport for when they did come after her.

Wycarri Prime was a surprisingly lush and temperate world. It was nothing like she had imagined it. Oh, she had listened to the briefings, but in her head, a race like the Mechi had no place living on a world like this one. The woods around her reminded her of Earth. If she wasn't in the process of running for her life, she would have taken the time to soak in the beauty surrounding her. There were very few places like these woods remaining on Earth. Overpopulation and progress changed the Earth a great deal from the world it once was. Most of the planet was industrialized now, countless cities stretching across its surface. For all the Mechi's apparent love of technology, the bugs had somehow managed to keep their world as it should be. That was likely because most of the Mechi population lived beneath the planet's surface in giant subterranean hives where most of their young were hatched and raised to adulthood. The population of Wycarri Prime was estimated to be over five times that of Earth's, yet only a small fraction of that number inhabited its surface and that was likely why woods like these had survived.

In the distance, far away, Wallace heard the sound of dropship engines howling to life. She stopped where she was looking up through the cover of the trees at the night sky. Standing there, Wallace watched the battalion's dropships racing upwards towards the planet's outer atmosphere. Her heart sank in her chest and her hopes died. Lieutenant Colonel Lyle had left her behind.

For him to do that meant the situation must have grown more dire than she would have thought possible. Then things got even worse. Several squadrons of Mechi fighters came screeching through the night sky from the west. The planet's primary spaceport was behind her to the north, so the fighters hadn't come from there. Likely, they had lifted off from some nearby Mechi military base.

The fighters closed in on the helpless dropships of the battalion, their forward cannons lighting the sky with blasts of bright death. She could see the orange flashes of tracer rounds speeding towards the dropships. One of the dropships exploded in a blossoming cloud of fire and light. It was only the first. Within the time span of a single minute, others followed it. Wallace fell to her knees, watching her soldiers die in the sky above her as the Mechi fighters ravaged the dropships in one wave after another.

It was all over as quickly as it began. A handful of dropships had gone spiraling back towards the planet's surface, leaving trails of flame in the air behind them as they went, but most had simply been blown to nothing by the Mechi fighters' assault.

Wallace closed her eyes as warm tears cut pathways through the grim and dirt smearing her cheeks. So many dead and for what? The tables had turned too fast for the battalion to have inflicted the sort of damage it had been meant to. Instead of breaking the Mechi's spirit by showing them that even their homeworld was vulnerable to attack by the forces of the Republic, likely the operation had only strengthened the Mechi's resolve to wipe the human race out of existence.

Her body shook with quiet sobs as Wallace wept for those that had died. She didn't know how long she sat there before she finally opened her eyes, but when she did, they were filled with determination. If this was to be the hand that fate dealt her, then she would make the most of it. In a moment of pure fury, she launched herself to her feet and activated the flamer unit on her wrist, hosing the trees around her. The intensity of the flames spewing over them caused them to catch fire themselves almost instantly. She watched them burn. The Mechi didn't deserve such beauty on their world. They had no right to it. No right at all. Later, she might regret using part of her flamers' limited fuel for something like this, but nonetheless, watching the trees burn brought her some comfort.

The bugs would surely see the flames and come to investigate what had caused them. Still, she lingered a few minutes longer, enjoying how the fire danced among the burning trees in the darkness of the night, before she started moving again.

Though the dropships were gone, she kept her course southward. In truth, there was nowhere she could go where the bugs wouldn't find her given time, so it seemed as good a direction to head in as any.

****

Krellman, Brent, and Gunter saw the death of the battalion's dropships high above the city to the south in the night sky, but it was the least of their worries. They were engaged with several squads of Mechi troopers on the outskirts of the capital. Brent "Metalface" Hyatt's tri-barreled weapon unleashed a barrage of high-velocity rounds at the bugs' position. One Mechi trooper's head exploded in an eruption of black pus. Another two fell, nearly cut in half by the blast as Brent ducked behind the cover of an overturned Mechi troop carrier.

Krellman took a turn, popping up from where he crouched to send another Mechi trooper to Hell. His shot plunged dead on into the center of the bug's armored chest, through armor and exoskeleton alike, to emerge from its back in a spray of shredded innards and blood.

Gunter was beginning to lose it. "We can't keep this up. I'm down to my last two mags."

Brent gave him a look of contempt and shook his head. "We fight until we die or we get the hell out of here. We'll do with it with our knives if we have to."

"It won't come to that," Krellman said with a wry grin. "I think I just spotted our ticket out of here."

Not far from their position sat what passed for a Mechi car. It was sitting, abandoned with its driver's door swung open. Krellman pointed at it. "Think either of you guys can drive that thing?"

"If it means getting out of here alive, I'll learn," Gunter said.

Gunter had done time on previous ops. as an A.P.C. driver before being transferred to join up with Krellman.

"Good," Krellman nodded. "Brent ..."

A twisted mockery of a smile stretched across Brent's half-metal, half-scar-covered face. The big man appeared to know exactly what Krellman wanted him to do. He leaped to his feet, a battle cry booming from the depths of his lungs, and hosed the Mechi troopers with his tri-barrel machine gun. The unexpected intensity of his attack sent the bugs ducking behind whatever cover they could find.

"Go!" Krellman said, shoving Gunter on ahead of him. The two of them broke from behind the overturned Mechi carrier, sprinting along the street towards the car. Gunter reached the vehicle first, lunging into its driver's seat. He fired it up as Krellman jumped inside beside him.

Brent came running after them. The bugs had worked up the courage to start shooting at them again. Bullets pinged off the asphalt of the street all around Brent as he ran. Krellman saw Brent take a hit, but the big man didn't slow down. Leaning out of the car and setting his rifle to full-auto, he returned fire at the bugs, trying to give Brent some cover fire. Empty shell casings flew from the side of his weapon to clatter onto the street below the car as Krellman emptied his mag. at the bugs then he dove into the rear of the car to give Brent room to get into it. Brent half-jumped, half-fell into the passenger seat that Krellman had just vacated, slamming the car's door closed.

"Hit it!" Krellman shouted at Gunter from the car's rear.

The car lurched forward, barely moving. Fire from the Mechi troopers racked over its side. Bits of glass from its exploding passenger-side windows rained over Krellman and Brent as they ducked.

"Frag it!" Brent screamed. He bled from numerous small wounds on his neck and upper back where tiny shards of the glass had torn into his flesh. "What the hell?" he raged at Gunter. "Get us moving already!"

"You ever tried to drive something that looks like it was designed for someone with more than two arms?" Gunter shouted back at him.

Gunter figured out at the "gas pedal" wasn't on the floor like in a human vehicle. It was on the dash next to the car's odd steering controls. He slammed a hand onto it and the car roared forward. Mechi fire continued to hammer into its rear as it went. The rear window shattered, raining more glass over Krellman who had sunk as far as he could to the car's floor.

The Mechi car plowed through the debris littering the road. It bounced about as it did so, tossing Brent around in his seat. Brent managed to catch himself with his right arm to keep his face from smashing into the car's dash. Gunter drove the car around the corner of the street and out of the Mechi troopers' line of fire.

"Thank God," Krellman muttered as the sound of the Mechi guns' grew more distant.

"Where to?" Gunter asked.

"South," Krellman said. "Out of the city."

"On it!" Gunter grinned as he kept the car's engine pushed to its limits.

****

Kurt could hear Shannon moving through the woods behind him. The little man creeped him out and with good reason. There was no doubt in Kurt's mind that Shannon was a serial killer. It was likely why Shannon joined up so that he could kill without breaking the law. Kurt shuddered as he saw the images of the bodies Shannon had mutilated in his mind. The man was a sicko and deserved to die or rather he needed to be put down for the good for every living thing. Right now though, Kurt needed him. Shannon seemed to be as talented with tech as he was at spilling blood. He might be the only real chance that Kurt had of getting off Wycarri Prime and seeing Diana again. Sometimes, the only thing you could do was make a deal with the devil and hope that devil didn't turn on you.

The smell of smoke was carried on the wind. Part of the woods was on fire not too far from where they were. Kurt stopped and took a look in the direction he believed it was coming from. Either the fire was too far away or the trees too thick between him and it for Kurt to see it.

"What is it?" Shannon growled, moving up to stand next to him.

"Don't you smell the smoke?" Kurt asked.

"What of it?" Shannon shrugged. "We're in a war zone. There's going to be smoke in places."

"This is close," Kurt argued. "Could mean the Mechi or some of our guys are close by."

Both of them had watched the battalion's dropships be blown out of the sky earlier in the night. They hadn't spoken about it, but they both knew what had happened. Shannon didn't seem to care. Kurt kept them heading south anyway. If one of the dropships had crashed after the Mechi fighters had made their run against them, it might just be salvageable. Kurt knew he couldn't repair a dropship even if they found one, but he would wager his soul that Shannon could. If they did find one and get it operating, they could finally escape the hell of Wycarri Prime. The *Hellbringer* had to be out there among the stars somewhere, waiting on

Lieutenant Colonel Lyle or whoever was left to call it in for extraction.

"We can't stand here staring at the trees all night," Shannon said. "If there are Mechi nearby either, we'll find them or they'll find us. It doesn't matter. I will not stand here and wait for death to find me."

Kurt nodded. He couldn't argue with Shannon's logic. "Don't suppose you want to take a turn on point?"

Shannon laughed. "I think you're rather doing a great job so far, Kurt. I see no reason to change things up."

Something moved in the woods to their right. Both Kurt and Shannon whirled towards the noise, their weapons raised and ready as a woman in Republic combat gear came stumbling out of the trees. She looked like she had been in some pretty heavy fighting. Her face and uniform were covered in dirt and grim. The woman was apparently as surprised by their presence in the woods as they were by hers.

"Who in the devil are you guys?" she rasped.

Shannon started to blow her away where she stood, but Kurt reached out to shove the barrel of his rifle towards the ground.

"I'm Kurt and this is Shannon," he said, "You'll have to forgive Kurt for being a bit trigger happy. We've had it pretty rough out here."

"Wallace," the woman said. "You heading south?"

Kurt nodded as hope swelled within him. Wallace looked like one tough mother and likely had to still be alive out here alone. If he could get her to join up with them, not only did he think she could handle Shannon if something set the little man off on a killing spree, but having her and the extra firepower she brought to the table was a good thing too. He had noticed the flamer unit on her wrist. She also had a matching set of pistols holstered on her hips.

"The dropships …" she started but Shannon interrupted her.

"We know, Wallace." Shannon's tone was harsh and cruel. "We saw them get blown to bits too."

Wallace's expression took on a hard edge as she and Shannon glared at each other.

"Heading south is still our best option though," Kurt interjected quickly. "If one of the dropships crashed in any kind of salvageable state, Shannon here is a tech genius. He might be able to get it flying again and get us out of here."

"He is, huh?" Wallace asked, sounding doubtful.

"I am," Shannon spoke up suddenly. Whether he was telling the truth or merely going along with his claim, Kurt didn't know. Shannon was clearly quick-witted, and Kurt could easily imagine him being a very skilled liar.

"We might as well head that way together," Kurt said. "Strength in numbers, right?"

"Not always." Wallace scowled, her eyes still fixed on Shannon.

A moment of silence ticked by as Kurt waited to see what Wallace was going to do.

"Sure, I'll go with you guys," Wallace said at last.

"Great!" Kurt smiled. Shannon said nothing, but Kurt saw him appraising Wallace even more intensely than he had been. Kurt was sure Wallace noticed it too.

"Lead the way then," Wallace told the two of them. "I'll bring up the rear."

****

"Dang it!" Gunter yelled. His fist smashed into the steering controls of the Mechi car. Its engine had given out, and it now sat unmoving on the dirt road, leading away from the capital city of Wycarri Prime.

"Ease up," Krellman said from the rear of the vehicle, reaching over the top of the driver's seat to place a hand on Gunter's shoulder. "It got us this far. At least we're out of the city."

"Will you two stop yakkin' already?" Brent growled. "We're sitting in the middle of an open road."

"Point," Gunter admitted, swinging the driver's side door to hop out of the vehicle.

The trio left the car behind, hurrying into the cover of the woods that surrounded the road. Once they hit the woods, they paused to get their direction and then started out southward. They had all seen the battalion's dropships die in a massacre as Mechi Fighters caught them before they could make it out of the planet's atmosphere. Krellman had been trying to reach Lieutenant Colonel Lyle or anyone really over the battalion's comm. net since then, but he hadn't any luck as yet. The Mechi were apparently jamming transmissions despite their victory.

"Still no luck making contact with anyone else?" Gunter asked, noticing his frown as they walked.

"Not a single peep out of anyone left alive out there," Krellman answered.

"There have to be others," Gunter said. "We can't be the only ones who lived through that crap in the city. And there were the units at the Mechi comm. center and spaceport too."

"We're alone," Brent grunted. "Deal with it."

"Do you have to be so negative?" Gunter challenged Brent.

Brent glared him and tapped the metal of his face with the fingertip of his right hand. "You live the life I have, kid, and you will be too."

"So if we're so sure everyone else is dead, why are we even bothering to head south then?" Gunter shook his head. "I mean, if we're going to die on this hellhole of a planet regardless of what we do, then why don't we turn around and take as many bugs with us as we can?"

"You're not a coward. I'll give you that." Brent chuckled.

"Because," Krellman spoke up, "there have to be other survivors. If we can find them and link up maybe, just maybe, all of us together can figure out a way home."

"Really?" Gunter stared at Krellman. "How? We gonna storm the spaceport and steal us a ride? I didn't even know you were a pilot."

"This from the guy who just asked our big friend over there to stop being negative?" Krellman smirked.

"Fine." Gunter shrugged. "Onward south we go then, but I still don't get the point of it all."

"Leave the thinking to your buddy," Brent snarled.

Gunter grunted at the rebuke but didn't take the chance of angering Brent by returning it. Brent "Metalface" Hyatt wasn't exactly known for his cool temperament and banter. Gunter was a big guy, but Brent was even larger than he was, and the cybernetic elements of his face were enough to put anyone on edge even if he seemed like a big, friendly giant. And he certainly wasn't that.

"This way, gentlemen." Krellman walked passed them, picking up his pace.

They walked for what seemed like hours before Gunter spoke up again. "Look, guys, I think it's time for a rest. My knees are killing me."

Krellman paused. "I could use one too. This seems as good a place as any to stop, I guess. The sun will be up soon anyway, and it might be better if we limited our movements to the cover of darkness."

"I'll agree to a rest," Brent informed them, "but we're not stopping for long. Time is against us, and our odds of living through all this get worse with each passing hour."

"You're right." Krellman nodded. "Sorry. I guess it's all catching up to me and I'm not thinking too clearly."

Gunter found a good spot to sit with his back leaning up against a tree and stretched his exhausted legs out in front of him. Krellman laid down flat out in the grass on his back, his gaze turned towards the heavens. Brent stayed on his feet though. He placed his heavy weapon against a tree close to him and stretched his arms upwards over his head as if trying to pop his back.

"I bet that thing really is heavy," Gunter commented, gesturing at Brent's weapon.

"It's worth the weight," Brent said.

Krellman dug into his backpack and produced a handful of ration bars. He tossed one to Brent and another to Gunter. "Don't know when we'll get the chance again," he told them, "and we all need the energy to keep going."

"You know these things taste like crap right?" Gunter laughed around the mouthful of his bar he had already stuffed into his mouth.

"Does he ever stop talking?" Brent asked.

"If he does, it's time to worry," Krellman answered, flashing Brent a grin.

"I'd kill for a burger and a beer right now," Gunter said, finishing up the last of his ration. "What about you guys?"

"Gunter," Krellman warned him, "I think our new friend would like you to shut up for a bit."

"Oh." Gunter looked over at Brent. "Sorry. I guess you figured out that I talk when I'm worried, huh?

"Just shut up for a few man," Krellman told him again.

"Sure thing," Gunter nodded and dug a canteen of water from his own pack. He twisted its cap loose and took a long, loud drink from it.

Krellman checked his chronometer. He planned to allow them a solid twenty-minute break before they got moving again. They all needed it, and more even Brent, no matter how tough the big man seemed. Looking over at Gunter again, Krellman saw that he had fallen asleep where he sat with his canteen still open in his hand.

The twenty minutes felt like it was over before it had even started to Krellman as he got to his feet. Brent was still standing, keeping a watchful eye on the trees around them.

Krellman walked over to Gunter and gave him a gentle kick to his side. "Time to wake up, sleeping beauty."

"Just another five, Mom," Gunter groaned up at him.

"On your feet, soldier!" Brent boomed.

Gunter's eyes sprang open and he leaped up like the world was ending.

Brent laughed. "That's better, kid. We need to get moving."

"Yes, sir," Gunter spat the words at him sarcastically.

"I got point this time," Brent announced.

Krellman shook his head. "No. I got it. Sorry, man, but I have the sharper eyes and ears."

"You really think so?" Brent pointed at cybernetic implant that was his left eye.

"Maybe not," Krellman admitted. "You got point then if you want it."

Without another word, Brent took the lead and plunged onto through the woods ahead of Krellman and Gunter.

****

Dropship 11 had been hit hard when the Mechi fighters attacked. Enemy fire had taken out her right engine, and she had gone into an almost uncontrollable spin, plunging towards the planet's surface, but she hadn't died in the air though like so many of the others. Lieutenant Alex Clayton lived up to his rep. of being one of the best dropship pilots in the Republic fleet and brought her in, hard, no choice there, but in pretty much one piece. The crash had knocked Clayton unconscious. He had no idea how long he was out before Corporal Marcus Waid's frantic shaking had woken him up.

Waid wasn't much more than a kid, fresh out of the academy with the shiny, new ranks bars of his rank on the sleeve of his uniform. Other than Clayton himself, Waid was the ranking officer of what remained of the platoon onboard Dropship 11. There were originally three others. A grumpy veteran named Spiker, a medic named Dodson, and a private named Henson. Waid had wanted him to take command, but he refused to do it. He wasn't a ground soldier, he was a pilot. Besides, command was never something Clayton has aspired to. All he wanted to do was fly. Clayton had been forced to take Waid aside and have a talk with him. It took some convincing, but Waid had reluctantly agreed to act as the C.O. of the survivors and let him skirt by as his second-in-command. That took the pressure off and Clayton felt worlds better for it.

Between himself and Waid, they quickly got everyone organized and decided on a course of action. Both he and Waid agreed that they needed to keep close to Dropship 11 and wait for help to come. The *Hellbringer* was supposed to be returning as their evac. According to the briefings on the Wycarri Prime op. Clayton hoped that when the *Hellbringer* found out just how much things had fallen apart on the surface, her crew would attempt a rescue mission to retrieve what survivors they could. Clayton admitted to himself that it was at best an unlikely hope, but it was the only one they had. So Waid and the others set up a defensive perimeter around the dropship while he went to work looking it over and trying to assess whether or not it could be fixed enough to reach orbit. The damage done by the Mechi fighters was bad but not so bad that Clayton thought the dropship would never fly again with a little luck and a lot of determination on his part. He wasn't an engineer, but he knew dropships and hoped he knew them well enough to get Dropship 11 airborne again.

Everything was going fine until the Mechi showed up. Dodson was the first to die as a blast of Mechi fire from some huge, cannon-like machine gun one of the bugs carried reduced the bulk of his body to nothing more than a spray of bone fragments and red mist. It was Spiker that saved all their butts then. The old man was the first to return fire as he yelled for all of them to take cover around the dropship. That had been over an hour ago.

Clayton cowered behind a stack of crates that the others had offloaded from the dropship, his pistol clutched tight in the sweaty palm of his hand. The last hour had been hell. It was taking everything he and the others had to just keep the bugs from overrunning their position. Dodson's corpse lay only a few feet from him. The medic had gone out in a moment of glory, dying as he lobbed a belt of grenades at the bug forces surrounding Dropship 11. His death hadn't been as gory to Clayton as Private Henson's had. A single bug round had burst through his skull, straight in, straight out. Looking at the mess of brain matter pooled around the young medic's body now though, Clayton felt sick. His other hand rose to cover his mouth as he struggled not to lean over and vomit into the grass. He knew if he did, he would likely die too.

Waid was wounded but not out of action. The kid had lived up to his training and then some, proving him worthy of the rank he had been given. It made Clayton sad to think the kid was would soon be dead. It all just seemed like such a waste. Waid had taken a round to his right shoulder that had fractured the bone there, and despite the slapped-on bandage the kid had smacked over the wound himself, Clayton knew the young corporal was bleeding out. The shots he took at the Mechi were erratic and lacked the carefulness of his earlier ones. The kid kept shooting though, and Clayton was glad for it. The stores of ammo onboard Dropship 11 gave them plenty of ammo to keep up the fight with as long as they were able to do it.

"Clayton!" Spiker shouted at him.

He knew it was time to do his bit again. Letting his pistol drop to the ground at his feet, Clayton hefted the RPG from where it sat next to him to his shoulder. Bracing it there, he leaped up from his cover and fired the heavy weapon into the trees. A patch of trees exploded, taking more than a handful of Mechi troopers with them. Clayton felt something sting him as he dropped back into a crouch behind the stack of crates he was using for cover. His side ached. As Mechi fire ripped into the crates behind him, he leaned against them and examined his wound. A bullet had grazed him, slashing open his flight suit and the skin beneath it. It could have been a lot worse and he knew it. Spiker and Waid, wounded as he was, were doing everything they could to hold the bugs at bay. Every time the bugs made a real push forward that the two of them couldn't handle, it fell to him to stop them. Four emptied RPG tubes littered the area around him. He only had one left. When it was gone, they were going to need a new tactic if they lived that long.

Spiker was using a belt-fed, tri-barrel machine gun. Clayton didn't even want to think about how belts of ammo Spiker had already worked through. Its barrels spun as Spiker used the distraction from the RPG's explosion to take out as many bugs as possible. The machine gun's fire raked the tree line north of the dropship's position. Bits of splintered wood flew from the trees as Mechi troopers between and behind them took multiple hits from the barrage of fire Spiker laid down on them. Clayton had no idea how many bugs they had killed by now, but it had to be a lot. One would think the bugs would have called off the attack by now or at least came up with a new plan for getting at them. Like worker ants though, the Mechi troopers simply continued on with the course they had set from themselves. If Clayton had been in command of the bug forces, he would have withdrawn and called in an airstrike on the dropship's position. Thankfully, the bugs hadn't done that so far. They couldn't possibly be so dumb as to not have thought of it, he figured, so therefore something else was keeping them from doing it. His best guess was that the bugs wanted prisoners so they could interrogate them and find out the reasons behind the attack on their homeworld.

Waid screamed, and Clayton's attention was jerked around in the young man's direction. He saw Waid's body lying in the grass. He could tell Waid was alive because the kid was still moving. How he was still alive was a whole other matter and one that was beyond Clayton. A burst of rounds had torn open the kid's guts. They spilled onto the ground like bloated, purple snakes slicked in red. Waid was trying to crawl towards Dropship 11 on his hands and knees, dragging his own innards along through the dirt and grass behind him. With Dodson dead, they were without a medic. Clayton desperately wanted to run to Waid and try to help him, but he was pinned down by Mechi fire where he was. He would never reach the kid if he tried. Clayton wondered for a second why Waid was trying to get inside the dropship. There was nothing within it that could help him. As Waid started up the dropship's ramp towards its open rear door, he suddenly realized exactly what Waid was up to. The kid was going to blow the ship so that the Mechi couldn't take it and gain access to the information in its logs. The blast would wipe out every Mechi trooper in the entire area, but it would take him and Spiker out too.

Clayton stared at Waid, watching the kid crawl up the dropship's ramp. The Mechi didn't seem to be targeting him. Their focus remained on the old veteran, Spiker, who was giving them hell and his own position where he crouched behind the stack of supply crates. The bugs apparently figured the kid wasn't a threat anymore, and their warped insectoid logic told them Waid was just seeking a better place to bleed out and die. That was bad. Bad for everyone. Clayton knew he'd die too if Waid made inside the ship. He couldn't let that happen. He wasn't ready to die yet, no matter how dire things were. Clayton thought about calling out to Waid, telling him to stop, but he knew Waid wouldn't listen to him if he could hear him which was unlikely given the cacophony of gunfire from the battle. He had to do something though.

Grabbing up his pistol, Clayton raised it at Waid and took aim at his young C.O. His hands trembled as he hesitated, despite knowing what he needed to do if he wanted to keep breathing. He shot a glance in Spiker's direction, but the old man didn't even appear to know what was going on with Waid. Spiker's attention was utterly focused on holding the Mechi troopers in the trees back from their position. That meant if someone was going to stop Waid, it had to be him. Clayton hesitated a few more moments hoping that the Mechi would take out Waid for him. They didn't.

Muttering a prayer for forgiveness, Clayton squeezed the trigger of his pistol. He was no marksman, but he got lucky. Waid's head snapped sideways as Clayton's round entered his skull just above his right ear. Flopping over, Waid's corpse rolled from the ramp into the grass and dirt below it.

Clayton sat there, paralyzed by the terribleness of his own action. He had just killed the young man he had put in charge of everyone after the crash. Mechi bullets continued to hammer into the crates he was using as cover, but he didn't hear them anymore. All he could do was continue to stare at Dropship 11's blood-smeared ramp.

Then, everything changed …

****

Krellman heard the sounds of the battle first, despite Brent being on point. He rushed forward as Brent heard them too and came to a stop. Gunter kept his position at the group's rear, watching the trees.

"Somebody's alive over there," Krellman said, "and really giving it to the bugs from the sound of things."

Brent smiled. "We should give them a hand then."

Krellman returned the smile and motioned at Gunter, signaling to him that they were going in. The three of them split up, approaching the battle from different angles. Brent charged forward through the trees while Krellman and Gunter broke, one to the right, one to the left.

Brent stopped as he came upon a mass of Mechi troopers in front of him. He had taken them completely by surprise. Clearly, they hadn't been expecting an attack to come from the rear of their position. The barrels of Brent's tri-barrel machine gun spun as he swept it back and forth over the bugs' ranks. One Mechi trooper tried to stand up from where it squatted. It staggered backwards as it was caught in Brent's stream of fire. Bullets blew chunks of its exoskeleton from its body, mangling its head, shoulders, and chest. Most of the bugs died where they crouched in the trees, bodies being flung over onto the ground, hissing and clicking in their death throes.

Krellman had swept around to the right. His approach was more cautious than Brent's. The bugs he came upon were turning towards the sounds of the chaos that Brent was causing as he reached them. There were only three of them, and they were in the process of erecting some sort of cannon-looking weapon. Krellman's rifle barked, blowing a hole clean through the largest of the three. Its body was picked up from the ground by the impact of the bullet tearing through it and flung several feet before flopping into the grass to lay still. The other two Mechi troopers went for their weapons, but Krellman was already on them. He swung the butt of his rifle upwards like a club, slamming it into the mandibles that covered the closest bug's mouth. One of the bug's mandibles cracked and bent to the side from the force of Krellman's blow even as Krellman swung the rifle around to smash its butt into the other bug's throat. The bug staggered backwards, making a horrid gagging noise. The other Mechi trooper had recovered from Krellman's blow to its face and was raising its weapon again as Krellman shoved the barrel of his rifle up against its forehead and pulled the trigger. The top of the bug's head vanished as the rifle's barrel flashed. Krellman spun towards the last of the three bugs again. His blow had done more damage than he had thought, caving in the bug's throat. It had dropped onto its four hands and knees, still struggling to breathe. Krellman opted not to waste a round on it. He kicked the bug over onto its back and used the butt of his rifle to cave its skull inward. Black fluid and brain matter leaked from its cracked-open head at Krellman's feet.

Gunter wasn't as lucky as his mates. He came plunging from the woods onto a group of bugs at the edge of the clearing they had surrounded. As he did so, whoever was alive in the clearing raked the area with a barrage of heavy fire. Two of the bugs took hits and dropped from it, but the remaining two managed to duck beneath one of the downed trees they were using as cover. Gunter, standing full upright, felt one round ripped at his left arm, leaving a gash spurting blood in its wake. A second bullet rammed into the center of the breastplate of his combat gear. It didn't penetrate, but it knocked the breath out of his lungs as it exited his body in a loud grunt. As Gunter fell, a third round stabbed into the meat of his upper right arm. He hit the ground with a thud. Gunter rolled away from the two bugs who had managed to take cover as they opened fire him. Bullets tore at the ground near him, sending chunks of dirt flying. He returned fire, his rifle on full-auto, spraying their position with wild, unaimed burst. One of the bugs gave a high-pitched squeal that sounded like the cry a dying pig might make. Gunter couldn't see if he had killed the bug or not. His focus was getting some cover between himself and the bugs before they opened up on him again. Leaving a trail of blood in the grass behind him as he went, Gunter crawled behind a tree and cowered there, not daring to attempt to get off another blast of fire at the bugs. He could barely hold his rifle as it was. Both his arms were wounded and the left was bleeding badly. He needed medical help and fast.

****

Clayton couldn't believe what he was seeing even as it happened. From out of nowhere, a group of Republic soldiers had shown up and attacked the bugs surrounding Dropship 11 from their rear. They'd done a good job of it too. Over a dozen of the bugs broke cover, running from the trees towards the dropship in an attempt to flee from whoever was hitting them from behind only to run smack into Spiker's line of fire. The old man swept his tri-barreled machine gun along the length of the tree line, cutting them to pieces as they ran.

As quickly as that, the tide of the battle had turned. Clayton leaned around the corner of the stack of crates he was using for cover and got into the action too. His pistol bucked in his hand as he shot a Mechi trooper that was charging towards him. The bug's charge from the trees ended as the force of the shot smacking into its face sent its body flipping over backwards.

A giant beast of a man with a gleaming metal face emerged from the trees, the large, tri-barreled machine gun in his hands tearing the last of the fleeing Mechi troopers to shreds, and then it was all over. Clayton stared at the man's horrid mockery of a human face as another Republic soldier stepped from the trees off to the west.

"Metalface!" Clayton heard Spiker shout. The old man left his own weapon, still smoking, where it sat, and ran to meet the newcomers.

The old veteran and the giant clasped hands.

"Spiker, you son of a ..." Metalface started, but the other soldier interrupted him.

"Where's Gunter?" Clayton heard him ask.

"Here!" a pained voice called from trees. A third soldier, badly wounded, came stumbling towards them.

"Gunter!" the man carrying the sniper rifle yelled and rushed to aid him.

"We thought we were dead," Spiker told the man with the metal face.

"Who's that?" The big man pointed at him as Clayton moved to join them where they stood.

"I'm Lieutenant Alex Clayton," he answered before Spiker could and then pointed behind him, "and that's my ship."

"You're a pilot?" the man with the metal face asked.

Clayton nodded. "I am."

"I'm Brent," the giant with the horrid face told him. "Those guys over there are Krellman and Gunter. Gunter's the one that's bleeding."

"I kind of figured that." Clayton looked up at Brent as the big man towered over him.

"Really glad you guys came along when you did," Spiker said. "I don't suppose there's an entire platoon following along behind you?"

Brent shook his head. "No. We're it. We've been on our own since the attack on the capital went to hell. Lucky we got out of the city alive."

"And you haven't run into anyone else?" Clayton frowned.

"You guys are the first we've run into … At least that are still alive," Brent added.

Spiker had left the two of them standing alone to go help the sniper with his friend's wounds. Spiker wasn't a medic, but Clayton knew he had seen enough battles to know what to do for anyone who was short of already being in the process of dying.

"That ship …" Brent gestured towards Dropship 11. "Can it fly?"

Clayton shrugged. "Maybe, given time and some work."

Brent laughed. "That's the best news I've heard today."

Spiker and the sniper, Krellman, helped Gunter aboard the dropship through its open rear door. As soon as they were inside it, Gunter made a show of shoving them away from him. Given the state of his arms, he failed.

"I think he's a bit delirious," Clayton heard Krellman say as he entered the dropship after them.

"He's lost a lot of blood," Spiker commented.

Clayton walked to one of the dropship's storage caches and tossed them a med-kit.

"Thanks." Krellman caught it up and flung it open. The first thing the sniper did was dig a long needle out of the kit.

"You're so not shooting me up with that," Gunter growled then broke into a deranged bout of laughter. "These are only flesh wounds."

Krellman stabbed the needle into Gunter's less wounded arm and plunged its top inward with his thumb.

"Hey …" Gunter called out, taking a weak swipe at the sniper with his left arm. Krellman caught his fist and held it.

"At ease, Gunter," Krellman ordered but Gunter had already slumped over as the sedative now coursing through his bloodstream hit him and knocked him out.

Spiker worked on stopping the blood flow from Gunter's nastier wound as Krellman bandaged the other.

Clayton watched it all with a smirk on his lips. Suddenly, he had hope that things just might turn okay after all.

****

Captain Reggie Tanner relished the burn of the whiskey as he swallowed his second shot. He slammed the shot glass onto his desk and left it there. Two was enough, more than enough really. There was much work to be done, and Lieutenant Colonel Lyle's entire battalion was counting on him. The pressure had gotten to him, but the whiskey had helped take the edge off it.

The *Hellbringer* had taken quite a beating from the Mechi fleet she had been forced to engage before being able to make the leap into Void space. His crew had worked nonstop at making the needed repairs to get her fully battle ready once more. They were pushed to limits just like he was. Mechi missiles had ripped holes in her sides, damaged her sensor array, knocked her sub-Void engines to around sixty percent of normal capacity, and taken out two of her portside launchers. She was in rough shape and that wasn't even considering the damage done to her shields. Their generators were nearly burned out from the strain they had been put under. On the upside, casualties were a lot less than they had any right to be. All total, only sixteen of his crew had died in the battle with perhaps twice that number wounded. Captain Tanner said a silent prayer of thanks for that.

A chime sounded from the doorway of his ready room. He looked up at the door, realizing that he was sitting in the dark; the glow of the data screen in front of him was the sole source of light in the room, casting long shadows onto its walls. He tucked the bottle of whiskey and shot glass inside the drawer of his desk and shoved it closed.

"Enter," he called out.

The ready room's door slid open and his XO, Thorson, entered.

"Captain," Thorson said, standing at attention.

"At ease and take a seat, Mr. Thorson," Tanner ordered.

Thorson moved to sit in the seat in front of Tanner's desk. "The sub-Void engine damage has been repaired."

"That's good news." Tanner smiled. "We could use a lot more of it."

"Indeed," Thorson agreed with a sharp nod.

"What is the status of the ship's shield generators?" Tanner asked.

"Not good. Sir." Thorson frowned. "Chief Burke is doing all he can, but it's unlikely that our shields will be at full strength when we return to Wycarri Prime."

"Has the courier drone been dispatched?" Tanner asked.

Thorson nodded again. "Yes, sir."

"That assures Command will know what happened out here if we don't make it home then," Captain Tanner said and then leaned forward in his chair. "The Mechi fleet that ripped us a new one wasn't supposed to be in the system when we arrived."

"I know, sir." Thorson's expression told Tanner that the XO was as worried as he was.

"To me, that says the Mechi must have been mobilizing for some sort of op. of their own." Captain Tanner shrugged. "We just showed up a bit too soon. If our arrival had been somewhat later, it's likely they would have already departed from the system. I suppose we can take comfort in the fact that our arrival had to have derailed whatever it was the bugs were planning."

"Maybe, sir, but odds are, they will be there when we return to the Wycarri system," Thorson pointed out. "The bugs will keep those ships close at hand now and likely recall other ships to strength the level of protection around Wycarri Prime. We'll have a hell of a time getting through them when we go back. And with our shields not fully functional …"

"I'm aware of the situation we're facing, Mr. Thorson," Captain Tanner said in a stern tone. "However, I am not abandoning Lieutenant Colonel Lyle and his battalion. We're the only hope that they have of extraction. If we wait for reinforcements, any action we take to get them out will surely come too late."

"Do you have a plan yet, sir?" Thorson asked. "With the damage our sensors took, it'll be difficult to know what we'll really be up against before we drop in system."

Captain Tanner spread his hands in front of him in defeat. "All we can do is drop in as close to Wycarri Prime as the *Hellbringer* can handle doing and hope for the best. We'll just have to hope that Lyle and his men will be ready for us."

"Whatever window we do have to get them out will surely be a small one." Thorson frowned.

"I want our two squadrons of fighters prepped and ready for launch as soon as we drop out of Void space," Captain Tanner ordered.

"Sir?" Thorson looked confused. He could see Thorson wondering why he had given the order. The man was likely wondering what good deploying two squadrons of fighters could possibly do against the size of fleet they were likely to find themselves up against.

"Make sure the pilots know the odds of them living through what I have planned for them are small. If you can, try to make sure whatever pilots are assigned to the mission don't have families waiting on them back home," Captain Tanner added.

"You're going to use the fighters as a distraction," Thorson blurted out as the realization of what Captain Tanner had in mind struck him.

"They're all we have, Thorson," Captain Tanner said. "They're not much, I know, but if they go howling out of the *Hellbringer*'s bays, weapons blazing …"

"They will give the Mechi more targets to shoot at than just us," Thorson said, understanding.

"With our shields crippled, that's my hope anyway," Captain Tanner confirmed. "And if they happen to inflict some notable damage on the forces we'll be facing, well, that would be fantastic."

"I'll make sure the pilots are properly briefed, sir," Thorson promised.

"Yes, see to it," Captain Tanner commented turning the data screen on his desk so that Thorson could see it. "I've been running simulations on deploying the fighters in such a manner. With them in play, our overall odds of survival this mess goes about by ten percent even in the worst case. My main concern is that Lyle and his men won't be ready."

"We'll begin broadcasting the rally signal as soon as we drop out of Void space, sir," Thorson said.

"We have no means of knowing how things went with the operation on the planet, Thorson." Captain Tanner longed for another shot of whiskey but wasn't about to pull out the bottle in front of his XO. Thorson was too much of a by-the-book officer for him to feel comfortable doing so. Instead, he raised a hand to his mouth and gnawed on one of his fingernails instead to help with the tension he was feeling. "It's possible that things went as badly on the surface as it did for us, maybe even worse."

Thorson said nothing, waiting on him to continue.

"If it did, there might not be anyone left for us to evac." Captain Tanner's frown grew deeper. "We have to try though."

"I know we do, so ..." Thorson glanced at the ready room's door behind where he sat. "I'd best be getting to it then sir. There's so much to do and so little time."

"Hold up a second longer, Thorson," Captain Tanner ordered him. "Remember to make sure that protocols are followed and there's an emergency courier drone ready."

Protocols dictated that such a drone was on active status at all times during combat mission. It was to be launched, if possible, to inform the powers that be back home of what they would need to know should the *Hellbringer* be destroyed and Captain Tanner unable to make such a report himself.

Thorson was all but vibrating in his chair with nervous energy, eager to get started on the tasks ahead of him. Captain Tanner decided to have mercy on the man, despite the fact that he didn't want to be alone.

"Dismissed," Captain Tanner said.

Thorson rose from his seat and exited the ready room leaving him alone in the dark once more.

"God help us all," Captain Tanner muttered and opened the drawer of his desk to reach for the bottle of whiskey he had tucked away.

****

Lieutenant Philip came out of the briefing room ready to go. He had listened to XO Thorson's grim layout of what lay ahead for him and the other pilots. Thorson had gone so far as to make the mission a voluntary one. Philip had been among the first to step up for it. The Xera fighter craft that the *Hellbringer* carried in its two bays were the most advanced ever developed by the Republic. They were small, insanely fast and maneuverable, and armed to the teeth. Each Xera fighter carried four ship-killer missiles in addition to its primary cannons. Usually, the fighters were deployed as a screen for whatever vessel they were launched from. Not this time. This time, they would be flying straight at the enemy. They were to strike at the Mechi fleet as hard as they could in the hopes of drawing fire away from the *Hellbringer* as the massive hybrid carrier/battleship entered orbit around the Mechi homeworld. The *Hellbringer* would pretty much be a sitting duck during the time it waited for whatever was left of Lieutenant Colonel Lyle's battalion on the planet's surface to achieve orbit in their dropships and meet it. Everyone aboard the massive ship knew just how badly her shields were still damaged. They would be at thirty percent of what they were on the *Hellbringer*'s last run at Wycarri Prime. And last time, the *Hellbringer* had barely gotten out.

"Cheer up, buddy." Elson laughed, slapping him on the shoulder as he caught up with him in the corridor. "We all have to die sometime."

"I ain't afraid of dying," Philip snarled, stopping to turn towards Elson.

Elson held up his hands in a gesture of peace. "Whoa, man, I didn't say that you were."

The anger vanished from Philip's expression as he reached out and clasped Elson by his shoulders.

"Elson, we've flown together for how long now?" Philip asked.

Elson shrugged. "I don't know. Maybe two years?"

"And we've lived through each and every launch, haven't we?"

Elson laughed again. "Sure, man," he answered, not knowing what else to say.

"Then there's no reason we can't make it through this one too, eh?"

"I guess not," Elson reluctantly agreed. "But ..."

"Shut up, Elson," Philip ordered him. "All we need to be focused on is taking out as many bugs as we can. Each and every shot is gonna matter out there. We have to make them count."

"Always," Elson said, staring at Philip as if he had gone insane. "You're acting really weird, man. You sure you're okay?"

"Wallace is on the planet," Philip said, as if those five words explained everything, and to someone who knew him as well Elson, they did.

"Holy crap, Philip. I didn't know," Elson blurted out. "I'm sorry, buddy."

"No," Philip snapped. "Don't tell me that you're sorry. There's no reason to believe that things went as badly on the surface as they did for the *Hellbringer*. I know she's okay, Elson. I have to believe that she is ... And we're going to clear the way for her."

"Totally, man," Elson said.

Philip and Wallace had dated for six months. He had taken their relationship very seriously. She hadn't. Relationships between officers in the marines and the fleet weren't unheard of, but they were rough on those involved. It was difficult to find time together around whatever missions duty called them to. Philip had done all he could to make theirs work though. At the end, he had asked Wallace to marry him. She had all but laughed in his face at the offer. He had loved her with every fiber of his being but what he had been to her, he couldn't guess. Sex? Stress relief? An escape from the weariness of military life? He truly had no idea. If she had ever loved him, she hadn't said so. He knew she felt something for him though, because even after that humiliating rejection, she had begged him to stay her friend. And he had, despite the pain in his heart each time he saw her with someone new. None of that mattered though. He loved her, and there was no changing how he felt about her for better or worse.

"Come on," Philip urged Elson. "Let's get suited up and to our fighters."

"Philip," Elson said, stopping him again. "We'll get her out."

He could see that Elson meant what he said. Elson was his closest and maybe only real friend in the fleet aside from Wallace. Elson's words only served to tighten up his nerves more, regardless of their intent. Philip was well aware that he might never know if Wallace made it off the bugs' homeworld or not, but he knew he would gladly give his life to buy her the time she and the other dropship troopers the chance to do so. He owed her that much for all the good times they had shared between them whether she had broken his heart in the end or not.

Philip turned away from Elson without saying another word to him and continued along the corridor.

****

Kurt rolled about on the grass of the woods beneath the combat jacket he was using as a blanket. His eyes darted about beneath closed lids and sweat slicked his skin.

Diana's scream echoed across the valley. Two bug warriors held her between them, dragging her along with them. Hundreds more separated him from her as Kurt's knuckles went white from the pressure of the grip his clenched fists held on the matching long swords he carried with. Without any hesitation, Kurt raced down the side of the hill he stood atop into the ranks of the bugs. Some of them carried rifles and those that did opened fire on him as he charged at them. Kurt's blades blurred as they danced in front of him. Their blades met the bullets aimed at him, sparking with each impact. His speed was inhuman, even godlike, as he batted the bullets from the air. Some of the bugs gathered in the valley recoiled in horror at the sight. None of the foul creatures broke ranks though.

Plowing into the bugs, Kurt's blades lashed out. Heads flew from shoulders. Arms were severed and exoskeletons ruptured. He gutted one bug, slashing its body open from the softer area between its legs to its throat. The bugs that held swords of their own closed in on him, trying to smother him with their numbers. Kurt remained relentless. He parried their blows and returned them, hacking away at one bug after another until he stood in the center of a great field of corpses. The black sludge of bug blood and sweat dripped from him and stained his blades. As intense and long as the battle was, he felt nothing but power coursing through his limbs.

The two bugs dragging Diana away had paused, staring at him with pure horror in their eyes. Nothing stood between him and them now. He threw one sword on ahead of him as he began to run towards them. The sword flew end over end through the air to embed itself into the skull of the bug to Diana's right. Its pincers released its hold on her as its corpse toppled to the ground. The other bug released Diana as well, drawing a curved sword from the scabbard that hung upon its hip.

The bug sprang forward to meet him. Its fear was gone and it grew in size with each step it took. By the time they met, it towered above Kurt. Their blades clanged against one another. Kurt's blades formed an X as he strained against the strength of the giant bug. It cackled wildly at him. Its laughter sounded much like a fingernail scratching along the length of an old Earth blackboard. The noise grew to a deafening level. Kurt was forced to break free of their struggle, dodging as the giant bug's blade was finally allowed to come down towards him. It struck the ground where he had stood, tearing it open. The fissure grew as the ground shook beneath Kurt's feet. When the shaking stopped, the fissure had grown to the size of a lake. Kurt stared across at the giant bug as the creature turned its back on him.

"No!" Kurt howled, unable to get across the fissure the bug had created, as the bug snatched Diana up from where it had left her. She was screaming and slamming her fists against the chitin of the massive hand that enveloped her waist. The bug raised her to its mouth, and with a single, quick motion, it bit her head from her body. Blood exploded in a geyser from the mangled stub of Diana's neck.

"No!" Kurt cried again to the heavens as he collapsed onto his knees and his swords slid from his hands.

Kurt awoke, throwing the jacket he had been using as a blanket aside. He looked at his own hand to see that he had drawn his sidearm and held it ready in his hand. His head jerked from side to side as he looked around the small clearing he and the others had stopped to rest in. There was no sign of Shannon or Wallace.

Wycarri Prime's sun was rising and its rays were beginning to shine through the cover of the trees above him where he sat.

Leaping to his feet, Kurt heard the sounds of a struggle nearby. He ran towards the noise, letting it guide his feet. The low-lying, thin branches of the trees slapped at his face, scratching his flesh and drawing blood. He ignored them, keeping his pistol ready as he lunged onwards through the woods.

Kurt burst into another small clearing to see Shannon sitting on top of Wallace. She thrashed about beneath him, trying to fight him off of her. Her balled-up fists delivered powerful blows to his chest and arms. Shannon grunted as each of them landed. The little man was unmoved, however, as if some demonic force gave him the power to take whatever needed to be endured to finish the task before him. Horrible gurgling sounds came from Wallace as she struggled under Shannon. The little man had sunk the blade of his knife into the center of her throat and was keeping pressure on it as Wallace died beneath him. Kurt wanted to scream for Shannon to stop, to do something to save Wallace, but he knew she was dead. Even if he knocked Shannon from her, the wound he had dealt to her throat was a fatal one that there was no coming back from.

Shannon made a sound too. It was akin to a man awash in orgasmic pleasure as Wallace finally stopped thrashing about and her arms fell limp to the grass of the woods. Slowly withdrawing his knife from Wallace's corpse, the little man licked at the blood staining its blade before he noticed Kurt.

"She was slowing us up and you know it," Shannon purred through blood-smeared lips. "I couldn't allow that."

Words failed Kurt as he stared at Shannon. He knew he could end the little man right there and then. Kurt's finger twitched on the trigger of his pistol, but he didn't raise the weapon at Kurt.

"Good news." Shannon smiled after wiping Wallace's blood from his lips with the backside of his hand. "I've found more of us alive."

"W-W-What?" Kurt stammered.

Shannon tapped the comm. on his helmet with the pointer finger of his right hand. "I said, I've found more of us alive, Kurt. I picked up a transponder signal from a Republic dropship. It just turned on, so logic follows that someone has to be alive wherever the dropship is to have activated it."

"Oh," Kurt said. It was all he could muster as a response.

Laughing, Shannon started towards him. "Come on now. I thought you'd be happier than that. There's a fair chance that if we can make it to that dropship, we can go home. I know how much going home means to you, Kurt. You are my friend after all."

"I'm your friend," Kurt repeated Shannon's words, feeling like he was going to vomit.

"Let's get some breakfast into us and get moving," Shannon beamed at him.

"Aren't … Aren't you at least going to bury her?" Kurt managed to ask.

"I don't see the point." Shannon laughed. "Besides, we don't have the time, remember?"

Shannon shrugged his backpack from his shoulders and dug through it. He handed Kurt a ration bar as he flung it onto his back again. "We've got to keep up our strength. Odds are, we're going to need it. I've figured out a means of using my comm. to trace the signal of the dropship's transponder. I believe it's less than two miles from where we are. If we double time it, we'll be there before you know it."

Gnawing on his own ration bar, Shannon strolled on by him, apparently heading in the direction of the dropship he claimed to have located. Kurt continued to stand where he was, staring at Wallace's corpse. He realized that he had become numb to the horror in front of him. The sight of Wallace's mangled throat and sprawled out body, resting in a pool of her congealing blood, had lost its importance to him as Shannon's words sunk into his brain. If Shannon wasn't lying, the two of them could really be on their way home.

"Come on!" Shannon yelled back at him, already well ahead.

The little serial killer's voice snapped Kurt out of his trance-like state. Something within him told him that he would never forget the sight of Wallace's corpse lying there on the ground before him, but he shook himself anyway to clear his head and rushed to catch up to Shannon.

"I left my rifle where we were sleeping," Kurt told Shannon.

"Go get it then," Shannon growled. "I'll wait for you but do hurry. I'm eager to meet whoever is waiting on us out there. In fact," Shannon announced, his lips parting in a demented grin, "I think I'll go back and get that woman's flamer unit while you do. Having more firepower at hand is never a bad thing."

****

87

"Ow!" Clayton shouted as he leaped away from Dropship 11's forward console. The wires he had been attempting to splice together had shocked the bloody fire out his fingers.

"It's not going well I take it," he heard Krellman ask from behind him. Clayton and the sniper had hit it off as soon as they had gotten a chance to talk. Krellman had volunteered to help him with the interior repairs to the dropship and Clayton had accepted his offer.

Krellman was as laid back as he was. The sniper had a good sense of humor, and his jokes when he made them weren't as annoying as his friend Gunter's. That guy rubbed Clayton the wrong way at times, but Clayton knew he meant well. The only one of the newcomers that really made Clayton uneasy was the giant with the metal face named Brent. Spiker clearly adored the giant and respected him, but Clayton just couldn't past the man's face. Brent's cybernetic eye disgusted Clayton most of all. It constantly burned an eerie shade of red that reminded him of a tiny light bulb on a strand of Christmas tree lights. The thing was just creepy. The intensity of the light it put out changed with Brent's mood. It was just so utterly inhuman. Like most everyone else in the Republic, Clayton scorned cybernetics in general because they were such a huge part of Mechi culture. Anything that the bugs loved so much couldn't be a good thing. Clayton felt bad about how he stared at that eye whenever Brent spoke to him. No matter how he tried not to, he ended up doing it anyway. There was no chance that Brent hadn't noticed him doing it too. Thankfully, the giant hadn't made an issue of it. Maybe Brent was used to being stared at.

Clayton rubbed his hands together trying to get feeling back into them. The shock he had gotten made them numb. In truth, he was dang lucky it hadn't killed him outright. He saw that Krellman was patiently waiting on an answer to the question he had asked. Clayton put on a smile and tried not to sound too negative.

"It could certainly be going better," he admitted at last.

"Cut yourself some slack," Krellman told him. "You're a pilot, not an engineer."

"I'm also the only chance we have of getting this ship in space," Clayton moaned, giving up trying to give their situation a positive spin.

"Take your time and do things right," Krellman advised him. "Rushing things will only get you hurt or worse, all of us killed when this ship does leave the ground."

"I just wish I had some help," Clayton commented.

"Hey now," Krellman said. "That's why I am here. You just haven't told me what I should be doing yet."

"Sorry," Clayton laughed. "I meant help that actually knows what they're doing."

Krellman frowned at him as Clayton moved over to the console again.

"You know what I mean," Clayton said. "If we had someone with us who really knew their way around these types of electronics, we'd be airborne by now."

Clayton returned to work, doing what he could to get the dropship operational as Brent entered the pilot compartment. The giant had to hunch over to get through the doorway.

"Your friend Gunter is as annoying as ever," Brent said to Krellman. "For a guy who took three rounds and stranded on the homeworld of his enemy, he's in fantastic spirits."

"That old guy is one heck of a medic, I guess," Krellman commented.

"He's not a medic," Clayton said.

"Sure could have fooled me," Krellman admitted.

"Spiker's been a ground-pounder for a long time," Brent told the sniper. "A man learns things on the battlefield when he has to."

"Anybody else starving?" Krellman asked.

"I could go for a steak," Brent said.

"I hear you." Krellman nodded. "More of a burger guy myself, but anything would be better than those craptastic ration bars."

Clayton stopped his work and smiled. "There are some MREs in the dropship's storage caches. They're not much better than the bars but ..."

"I'm in for one of those. You want one, Krellman?" Brent offered as he turned around to head back out.

"I'm good," Krellman assured the giant.

Brent paused awkwardly in the doorway between the pilot's compartment and the dropship's rear. "Oh," he said, "I forgot to ask. We got any kind of E.T.A. on when we'll be flying out of here yet?"

Clayton shook his head sadly. "Not yet, but you'll be the first to know when we do."

"The bugs have to know this dropship is out here," Brent told them. "They'll be coming sooner rather than later. You can count on that."

"Have Spiker get outside and keep an eye on the woods. Clayton has the sensors online, and the last scan I ran of the area showed that the area is clear of them at the moment. Like you said, that could change in a heartbeat though. Better to be safe than sorry."

"I'll get Spiker out there," Brent promised and then disappeared into the dropship's rear.

"What I can't figure out," Krellman shrugged, "is why the bugs didn't just blow this ship to hell from the air and be done with it."

"Yeah," Clayton agreed. "It's what I would have done in their place. Maybe there are other groups like ours still out there keeping the fight going and we're just not a priority for them yet."

"That makes sense," Krellman said. "I hope that's the case too because if not, our time may be a lot shorter than we even think it is."

Clayton finally managed to splice the two wires he was fiddling with. The shuttle's helm controls lit up and came to life on the console above him. "Oorah!" Clayton shouted, surprised by his victory.

"Careful, flyboy," Krellman warned him, "I think you're spending too much time around a bad crowd of people."

The burst of laughter that erupted from him shook Clayton as he smiled at Krellman. "You could be right."

Clayton double-checked to make sure his patching was going to hold. "I think I got that fixed up pretty well. Now if I could just figure out how to run the bypass I need to do in order to get power from the ship's engines."

"We have power." Krellman pointed at the lights on the console.

"That's battery power you're seeing," Clayton told him. "That's keeping things on right now, but it's nowhere near enough to get us airborne much less into orbit."

"Okay." Krellman shifted his position in the copilot seat. "Guess you need to figure out how to do that then, huh?"

"Tell me about it," Clayton groaned.

****

As Wycarri Prime's sun reached its high point in the midday sky, Kurt and Shannon crouched in the trees, hiding, as a trio of Mechi soldiers moved through the woods not twenty feet from their position. The bugs didn't know they were there or the shooting would have started already.

Kurt had managed to escape a Mechi patrol once before since the battalion's mission on the planet had fallen apart, and he had ended up on alone and on the run. He didn't think he was going to be so lucky this time. One of the Mechi troopers had a cybernetic hand, shaped much like a human's, except that its fingers ended in odd, antenna-looking digits that spun slowly about as the bug walked. The things looked like they were the Mechi equivalent to the handheld scanners that Republic soldiers sometimes carried when on patrol. All the bug had to do was accidently point it in their direction, and it would know the two of them were there.

"We need to take them out," Shannon whispered.

Kurt couldn't argue with the little serial killer's logic, though he did wonder if Shannon wanted the sport of killing the bugs more than he cared about whether or not they would be discovered.

Shannon moved slowly and quietly through the brush away from him. Kurt wondered where in the devil the little man was heading for. Then, he saw what Shannon was trying to do. Shannon crept towards the rear bug that made up the trio of the patrol. His knife was out and in his hand.

When Shannon was in position, he gestured at Kurt. Kurt knew Shannon wanted him to open fire on the other two bugs. With a bit of luck, he might be able to take both of them before either was able to fire a shot and Shannon would deal with the third, his way. Kurt wasn't a fan of the plan Shannon had just came up with on the fly, but he had no other option except to wait for the bugs to discover they were there. And the bugs surely would too. Even now, the Mechi trooper with the odd fingers swept them back and forth, getting ever closer to pointing them at the spot where he crouched.

"Hell with it," Kurt muttered. He leaped to his feet, the barrel of his rifle leveled at the two closest bugs. The rifle chattered and bucked in his hands as he sprayed the two bugs with a stream of fully automatic fire that sent them reeling. They died on their feet as his bullets hit them before they even so much as realized what was happening.

The third bug swung its weapon towards him and Kurt's eyes went wide. He knew he would never be able to bring his rifle around in time to stop the bug from firing if Shannon failed to do his job.

Shannon came bounding from the trees behind the last bug and tackled it. The two of them hit the dirt of the forest floor hard. Shannon's knife rose and fell in rapid succession. A spray of black blood squirted upwards each time it descended. Shannon was howling with rapture-like glee as he continued to stab the bug long after it had stopped moving.

"I think that's enough," Kurt called to him, leaving the cover of the trees to approach the little man. "It's dead."

Shannon looked up at, his lips twisted into a feral smile. "I do believe you're right. Forgive me if I got a touch carried away. It's also best to be sure I finish," Shannon told him.

"Any idea what these bugs might be doing out here?" Kurt asked.

"Looking for us perhaps," Shannon offered as a possible explanation.

"I doubt it." Kurt shook his head. "They did seem intent on finding something, but from how they were acting, it sure looked to be a great deal more important than just us."

"Give me a few minutes and I can find out." Shannon grinned.

"Do I even want to know how?" Kurt scanned the trees, looking around to make sure there were no more bugs close by.

"Mechi brains aren't entirely biological in nature." Shannon started work at cutting open the head of the bug he had just stabbed to death. "They have a cybernetic element to them. If I can extract that intact, it's really not more than a small data core."

"And you can hack it," Kurt realized.

"Of course," Shannon said with great pride.

"Fine." Kurt gave him a nod. "But don't expect me to watch."

"Just don't wander too far, Kurt," Shannon warned him. "These woods are a very dangerous place."

Shannon's warning sound very much like a veiled threat. The little serial killer appeared to have grown rather attached to his company, apparently even thought of them as friends. Kurt had no doubt that if he tried to leave Shannon behind, the little man would track him and end him. Leaving Shannon wasn't an option anyway as far as Kurt was concerned. He had made his deal with the devil and he was going to live with it. There was no backing out now. Even if he wanted to, he couldn't. Only Shannon knew where the dropship whose transponder signal they had detected was. Finding it and hopefully escaping this hellhole of a planet was all Kurt cared about.

Kurt left Shannon to his gory work and walked through the trees, looking up at the sun in the sky. When he felt had gone as far as he could without making Shannon suspect he was making a break for it, Kurt stopped. He traded out the half-spent magazine in his rifle for a fresh one and then propped the weapon against a tree so he could check the magazine of his pistol too. Anything to keep his mind off the things he had seen Shannon do and knew would do whenever they reached the dropship they were heading for. There was no doubt in his mind that Shannon's motivation for reaching it was different than his own. The only thing that seemed to drive the little man was killing, and Kurt knew Shannon preferred killing humans much more than killing the Mechi.

Sliding his pistol into the holster on his hip once more, Shannon picked up his rifle. It didn't bring him much comfort, but holding it was better than nothing. His grip on it grew tighter as he thought about what he was going to have to do when they did reach the dropship. He swore to himself that he would put Shannon down then like the mad dog the little man was. It wouldn't bring Wallace back from the dead or any of Shannon's other *who knew how many* victims, but it just might let him be able to sleep at night when he did make it home. Kurt knew he would never be able to tell Diana about Shannon and the things he had allowed the little serial killer to do in order to get home to her. She would never understand.

"All done," Shannon said proudly as the little man came bounding up to him from behind. Shannon held a black blood-smeared piece of metal in his hand. As Kurt looked at it more closely, he could see that the piece of metal had tiny wires dangling out of it.

"Throw that thing away," Kurt ordered Shannon, trying to hide the disgust he was feeling. He knew the piece of metal was part of the Mechi trooper's brain.

"I thought you might like to see it. It is a rather fascinating bit of hardware." Shannon frowned and then tossed the piece of metal away. "No matter, I suppose. To each their own."

"What did you find out from it?" Kurt asked.

"Those Mechi were indeed not looking for us at all. They were heading to the very spot we are." Shannon beamed. "And they're not alone either. It seems they were stragglers of a rather large group of Mechi troopers who have been tasked with securing and taking prisoners from the dropship we're headed to."

"So there are other Republic soldiers alive at the dropship," Kurt said as he felt his hopes of getting off Wycarri Prime rising even more than they had when Shannon first detected the dropship's transponder signal.

"Yes," Shannon confirmed. "The Mechi believe there are at least five survivors defending it."

"Then we really need to get moving. We have to beat the bugs to it," he almost shouted.

"The route the bugs are taking was in that piece of brain you had me cast aside. Thankfully, I was able to pull up a map of the area as well, and taking into account the strength of the dropship's transponder signal, I was able to find us a faster one." Shannon was on the verge dancing at how well he had done.

"You lead then," Kurt urged him. "It's time you took a turn on point anyway. I've had it the whole way so far."

"Don't mind if I do." Shannon smirked at him and darted away.

"Hey!" Kurt yelled and then started running after him. The little guy was faster than he looked.

****

"Shouldn't you be upfront helping your new buddy?" Gunter asked as Krellman took a seat next to where Gunter sat on the floor, leaning against the wall of the dropship's rear compartment. "The two of you really seem to get along."

"Is that a trace of jealousy I hear in your voice?" Krellman smirked.

"You know, you snipers are so full of yourselves it's a wonder I put up with you." Gunter cracked his knuckles. The movement must have sent pains shooting up his wounded arms because he winced and muttered a curse under his breath.

When Gunter's pain subsided, he asked, "So we any closer to getting home yet?"

"Depends on how you look at things, I guess." Krellman shrugged. "We've got a ship, it just isn't working."

"Could you pass me some water?" Gunter asked, changing the subject away from the topic of whether or not they were going to survive. "I'm getting mighty thirsty sitting over here on my butt doing nothing."

Krellman retrieved a bottle of water from one of the ship's storage caches and screwed off its top before handing it to Gunter. "Be glad you're even alive," Krellman said, trying to remind him of how lucky he was. "Not everybody who takes as many hits as you did is able to walk away from it."

"You miss anything, Krellman?" Gunter asked.

"I'm not sure I know what you mean." Krellman gave Gunter a look of concern.

"I miss how it rains on Earth," Gunter told him. "When I was a kid, I used to lay in my bed listening to it hit the roof of our house. It used to lull me to sleep. One night though, it really hammered the roof, like heaven itself had opened up its floodgates. Mom always told me that when it rained, the angels up there were crying. I'd like to hear rain like that one more time before I die, buddy."

Krellman rolled his eyes, pretending to be sickening by what Gunter had just told him. "First you're jealous and now you're going all sentimental on me. Maybe it would have been better if you had gone out in a blaze of glory after all."

"Shut up, Krellman," Gunter snapped at him. "You know what I mean. You have to admit, our odds of making it off this planet are next to nothing. Even if you guys get this hunk of junk airborne, what's to stop the Mechi from sending in fighters to shoot it out of the sky?"

Before Krellman could answer, Spiker poked his head into compartment where they were through the dropship's open rear door.

"We've got company coming," the old man warned.

Krellman sprang to his feet, grabbing up his sniper rifle. "You stay here," he ordered Gunter. "We got this."

Gunter threw his hands up in the air despite the pain that surely hit him from doing so and said, "Trust me, I ain't moving, buddy."

Krellman walked cautiously down the ramp leading out of the dropship to where Spiker stood waiting on him.

"Whoever it is, they're coming in fast and all stupid like," Spiker grunted.

"Bugs?" Krellman asked.

"Don't think so." Spiker spat into the dirt at his feet. "Even they ain't that dumb."

Krellman and Spiker took cover, settling into firing positions, as they aimed their weapons at the trees to the East.

A thin, pale little man emerged from the trees. He was waving his hands about frantically. "Don't shoot! Don't shoot!" he cried out. "We're not bugs."

Another man burst into the clearing after him. To Krellman, this second guy looked he had been through Hell and back. The expression he wore was a tight one and one that told Krellman the man was either about to break from the stress he must be under.

"Identify yourselves," Spiker ordered the two men.

"My name's Shannon and my friend over there is Kurt," the little man yelled at them.

Krellman found it odd that the little man had not used their ranks or designations but rather just their names. Something seemed out of whack about him to even if he did appear to be holding up better than his stressed-out friend was.

Krellman lowered his rifle, but Spiker didn't. The veteran kept his trained on the pair as Krellman got up from where he had taken cover and walked towards them. "How did you know we were here?" Krellman asked.

"Picked up the encrypted signal from that dropship's transponder," the little man, Shannon, answered.

Shannon's answer surprised Krellman and confused him. "How?"

"I modified my helmet's comlink so it could trace the signal and we followed it here," Shannon removed his helmet and held it out for Krellman to look at.

"You're an engineer?" Krellman asked, trying to hide the excitement that was growing inside him.

"No," Shannon answered.

"But he's a genius with tech," the other man, Kurt said, speaking up. "Any kind of tech. If it's broke, he can fix it."

Krellman turned to shoot Spiker a look of disbelief.

The old veteran snorted and finally lowered his weapon. "Glad to meet you boys then." Spiker laughed. "We've got some work for you."

****

Kurt sat on the dropship's ramp. The M.R.E. that sniper had given him tasted like heaven. It was just a simple meal of chicken and rice but compared to ration bars or nothing at all, it deserved the praise he gave it. A wounded man named Gunter had joined him on the ramp while he ate.

"So the dropship you rode in on crashed, huh?" Gunter said, trying to start up a conversation. Kurt didn't really want to talk. He just wanted to enjoy his meal in peace. Gunter was either oblivious to that fact or didn't care. Talking meant he might slip up and tell them about Shannon and the things the little man had done. Kurt had promised himself he would deal with the little serial killer when they found the dropship. He hadn't counted on the ship being damaged and only Shannon having the skill to fix it. If he blew the whistle on Shannon now, there was no telling what the others might do to the little man. All Kurt could do was keep his mouth shut until the dropship was repaired. He shoveled another spoonful of chicken into his mouth and ignored Gunter's question.

"I bet that sucked," Gunter commented when he didn't answer. "And then, you met up with the little guy, right?"

"This chicken is fantastic," Kurt said in an attempt to change the subject.

Gunter's expression was one of disgust. "You must really be hungry, kid, if that crap tastes good."

Kurt finished up his meal and sat the plastic tray he had eaten it from beside him. "Your friend, Krellman, he's a sniper and you're what, his spotter or something?"

"Or something." Gunter grinned.

"Is he in command here?" Kurt asked.

Gunter looked surprised. "I didn't realize it, kid, but I suppose he is. He's taken charge of things anyway."

"He's not the ranking officer?" Kurt glanced over the old man, Spiker, who was heading into the trees to resume his watch since he had apparently finally decided that he and Shannon weren't a threat.

"Clayton, the pilot of this piece of junk, has the highest rank I think." Gunter shrugged. "I'd wager he just isn't the command type or something. He sure let Krellman take over without question when we got here, that much I can tell you."

"And you trust Krellman to get us out of here?" Kurt pressed.

"I've trusted him with my life for a while, kid. He hasn't screwed me over yet," Gunter assured him.

Gunter looked him over for a long moment. "This is your first combat drop, isn't it?"

"What makes you think that?" Kurt countered him with a question for a question.

"You just seem a little green around the edges," Gunter answered. "Just kind of figured it was, ya know?"

"It's not," Kurt corrected him. "It's just the worse."

"I didn't mean any offense, kid," Gunter said carefully.

"Then stop calling me kid," Kurt told him. "You're not that much older than I am."

It was Gunter's turn to change the subject. "I can see you got someone waiting on you back home." Gunter gestured at the wedding band Kurt wore on his left hand.

"I do," Kurt nodded. "Her name is Diana."

"Must be hard." Gunter frowned and then added, "For you and her both."

"She's safe," Kurt said. "I made sure she moved onto a base before I shipped out."

"What world are you from?" Gunter asked. "I know it ain't Earth. I can tell."

"Wellhem IV," Kurt answered.

Gunter whistled. "That's one tough planet. I've heard things are falling apart there with the war."

"That's why I made sure she moved onto the base." Kurt met Gunter's eyes. "I couldn't have left if I …"

"It's okay, man," Gunter told him. "I get it. I mean, at least as much a guy like me can. I never got married. Don't know if it's because I haven't met the right woman yet or I'm just scared of being tied down."

A moment of silence ticked by before Gunter spoke again. "You're lucky in that you got someone to go home to. Most of us don't."

"I don't feel lucky," Kurt admitted. "Every hour I am away from her is pure torture."

"I can tell you really love her. It's written all over you, man." Gunter rubbed at his chest as he grimaced, clearly in pain.

"You want me to help you back into the ship?" Kurt asked.

"No. I'm fine." Gunter appeared to get himself together. "Took a round to the chest when my arms got shot up. Bruised it pretty bad even through my armor. No cracked ribs or anything according to Spiker. He checked me over good when the shooting stopped. The old man may not be a medic, but he seems to know his stuff. Guess he's like your friend in that regard, eh?"

"My friend?" Kurt asked and then realized that Gunter meant Shannon. "Oh, you mean Shannon. Yeah. I suppose he is like that too. He's not an engineer officially, but he should be given the things I've seen him do with just jury-rigged tools and his helmet's comlink."

"Clayton's been doing his best to get this bird here into the sky. Maybe between the two of them, they'll get it sorted out." Gunter tried to get up but looked to be having a lot of trouble doing so.

Kurt got up and helped him to his feet.

"Been good talking with you, kid," Gunter snorted. "But I think I had better get out of your way. Now that you've got some food in you, I imagine the more eyes we have out there in the woods keeping lookout for the bugs, the better given that you guys said there were a bunch of them headed this way."

"Shannon said he did something to slow them up," Kurt said. "I know he was messing with his comlink almost all the whole time we were running to get here."

"I guess he's okay by me then," Gunter said with a nod and a final grin before he disappeared into the dropship, leaving Kurt alone standing at the end of its ramp.

No, Kurt thought, *No, he's not okay at all.*

The memory of Wallace's mangled throat surfaced in Kurt's mind. He could recall every detail of how her corpse had looked as they had left it lying in the grass for whatever bugs that found it to make a meal of. Kurt shuddered as a chill ran along his spine. With a great deal of mental effort, he reminded himself that he was supposed to join the old man on watch and walked towards the trees surrounding the clearing that Dropship 11 sat in.

****

"That does it," Shannon told them as he emerged from the open hatch that contained the access to Dropship 11's engines. "Try it now and see."

"Shannon says to fire her up!" Krellman called from where he stood over Shannon to Clayton in the pilot's compartment, and Shannon leaped up out of the access area.

Dropship 11's engines roared to life, and the lights on its ceiling above them became brighter as more power coursed into them.

"Yeah baby!" Krellman heard Clayton shout from the dropship's pilot seat. "We're ready to rock and roll!"

"Great!" Krellman shouted back at him then turned to Shannon. "Good work."

"Happy to be of service." Shannon smiled. "I'm just glad it was such an easy fix."

"Don't tell Clayton how easy it was." Krellman laughed. "I thought he was going to have a stroke from trying to figure it out."

"Right then," Shannon said too seriously, "I shall endeavor not to."

"Okay," Krellman said awkwardly. "You get up there, Shannon, and do what you can to help him run whatever preflight checks he needs to do. I'll get the others."

Krellman darted towards the dropship's open rear door eager to get everyone inside and the ship in the air. He passed Gunter on the way. His old friends shot him a thumbs up as he went by.

As he reached the rear door and stepped outside it, Krellman stopped dead in his tracks. Something was wrong. He could feel it deep in his bones. The woods around the dropship weren't just quiet. They were eerily silent, like the calm before a storm. The hair on the back of his neck stood up as he ever so slowly backed up the way he had come. His rifle was propped against the dropship's wall just inside its open, rear doorway. Krellman reached for it as gunfire erupted in the woods outside. He threw himself to the side of the dropship's open door, using its frame as cover. Mechi bullets pinged against the hull of Dropship 11.

"We've got company!" he shouted towards the pilot's compartment.

Gunter, who was sitting in the rear compartment, still hindered by his wounds, tried to reach for his own rifle.

"Don't you even," Krellman warned Gunter. "I got this!"

"That kid and Spiker are still out there," Gunter reminded him. "We can't just leave them to die."

Letting loose a litany of curses, Krellman leaned around the edge of the open doorway and tried to get a look at the woods around the dropship without getting his head shot off his shoulders. There was no sign of the kid, Kurt, or the old veteran. If either of them were still alive, they sure as hell weren't engaging the bugs that were starting to spill into the clearing from the trees.

"Get that door closed back there!" Krellman heard Clayton shouting from the pilot's compartment. "We need to get airborne before those bastards accidently shoot something that matters!"

Krellman looked over at Gunter; he was busy doing something odd with a roll of duct tape to his arms. His old friend gave him a sad shrug as if to say there was nothing for it. It was the job. People died no matter what you did. All you could do was save those that you could and hope you made it out too. Krellman wanted to dash from the dropship, killing as many bugs as he could as he went, find the kid and the old man, and get them onto the ship. He knew if he did though that he would likely be just as dead as they probably already were. He smashed a clenched fist into the dropship's wall next to him in helpless frustration and then yanked at the lever that closed the dropship's ramp.

Without warning, Gunter plunged through the closing doorway passed him. Gunter had taped his arms in place so that they would stay up where he could hold a weapon in each hand. He clutched his pistol in one and his rifle in the other with tape stretching from where it was wrapped around his shoulders to his arms just between his hands and elbows.

"Time to bring the rain!" Gunter yelled as a battle cry as he jumped through the dropship's closing doorway. His rifle and pistol were firing continuously in rapid succession as he landed on his feet and ran towards the trees.

"Gunter! No!" Krellman screamed starting after him, but the dropship's ramp rose into place blocking his way as the Mechi troopers outside continued to fire on the dropship. Krellman could hear Gunter returning fire at them.

The second the door had fully closed, the floor under his feet shifted as the dropship lurched upwards from the ground. Krellman stumbled as he crashed into the closed-up rear door with a grunt of pain.

"Better get strapped in back there!" Clayton shouted from the pilot's compartment. "It's going to be a hell of a bumpy ride up!"

Tears welled up in Krellman's eyes as he staggered across the rear compartment to the closest safety harness and activated it. Its straps closed around him, holding him in place as he began to cry. Gunter had always acted the part of the hero, and now his old friend was going to die one too, alone, hopelessly outgunned and outnumbered.

****

Gunter had charged out of the dropship with his guns blazing. The tape he had used to get his wounded arms to function, like he needed them to, was holding so far. He didn't know for sure if he had hit any of the bugs or not, but he had certainly given them pause. He was able to find cover behind a stack of crates unloaded from the dropship before they really started shooting back at him. Gunter knew he couldn't stay behind them though. The bugs were serious about stopping the dropship from taking flight and were pouring into the clearing by the dozens. They would overrun his position, and with how many of them there were, he had no means of stopping them.

Gunter ran from the cover of the stack of crates, making for the trees on the other side of the clearing. He took comfort in that his mad charge from the dropship had bought Clayton the time he needed to get it into the air. Dropship 11 roared upwards towards the sky even as Gunter ran. He let out a victory cry as its engines kicked into high gear and its speed picked up. A Mechi bullet clipped his right thigh. Somehow, by the grace of God, he stayed on his feet. Gunter ignored the pain and kept running as blood flowed down the leg of his pants. He had done what he had intended to do and made sure the dropship got away. That had been his primary goal. His secondary goal was finding out what happened to Kurt and Spiker.

Gunter didn't dare try to return fire at the Mechi troopers he ran. If he so much as hesitated, he would be dead. He made it to the trees on the far side of the clearing and entered them. Just as he had hoped, there were no bugs waiting on him there. He dove behind a large tree. Half a second later, the bark on its opposite side was shredded and splintered by Mechi bullets. Gunter cursed as he sprinted deeper into the woods. He doubled back, running around the circle of the clearing, keeping the trees between him and the bullets that continued to fly in his direction. Gunter yanked a grenade from his belt and tossed into the clearing. He heard several bugs squealing and hissing in the moment before it exploded.

The Mechi troopers were in a disorganized and in a state of chaos. They had expected to be going up against a stationary target, not someone on the move. Gunter used that to his advantage and hoped his luck would hold.

At the far rear of the bugs' ranks, he saw two of them dragging a body along between them. It belonged to Spiker. The old veteran's head was half-gone. From the looks of it, a round from a high-powered, sniper-style weapon had taken out the old man before he was able to warn the dropship that the bugs were coming. He still didn't see any sign of Kurt but something deep within him told him that the kid was dead. He felt bad for Kurt. The kid had wanted to see his wife again so badly. Love like that was a rare and precious thing. Too bad love didn't count for crap on a battlefield.

Gunter's right leg gave out underneath him and sent him rolling through the grass. He bounced across the ground, carried along by his own momentum. When he finally stopped rolling, Gunter moved to get to his feet, hurling himself up. As he did so, a bullet slammed into his side. He felt it tearing through his innards as he howled like a dying animal. The tape holding his right arm up and in place snapped. That arm flopped to hang uselessly at his side as his rifle slipped from his grasp.

Two Mechi troopers were running towards him as he lay in the grass, bleeding out. Apparently, the two bugs wanted a prisoner they could question because they weren't shooting at him as they came.

The woods were swirling around him as Gunter managed one last, final act of defiance. He raised his pistol at the two approaching bugs and emptied its mag. at them. His aim was off, both from his distorted vision as he fought to stay conscious and the awkward angle the tape held his left arm up at with him lying in the grass. Still, he saw one of the bugs fall, black blood spraying from a crack in the exoskeleton of its upper body. The second bug reached him, knocking his pistol from his hand. Gunter kicked up at it with his good leg. His heavy combat boot made contact with the joint of its right knee. The bug squeaked and fell onto the grass next to him. Gunter rolled on top of it, sliding his knife out of the sheath strapped to his boot. He plunged its blade between the mandibles that protruded in front of the bug's open mouth. They clamped shut on his arm even as the blade of his knife entered the bug's mouth and sunk into the back of its throat. Gunter endured the pain with gritted teeth as he jerked his arm free, leaving the knife inside the bug. He flopped over onto his back, too weak to move anymore as the darkness claimed him. With his last thought, he hoped whatever bugs ate him choked on the flesh of his corpse.

****

Captain Tanner drummed his fingers on the arm of his command chair. The time to return to the Wycarri system had come. Ensign Sommers had taken Ensign Buchanan's place at the newly repaired communications station. Captain Tanner shuddered at the memory of Buchanan burning on the floor of the bridge, her body engulfed in flames from where the station had blown during the *Hellbringer*'s brief confrontation with the Mechi fleet. Though he knew the stench of Buchanan's smoldering hair and cooking flesh existed only in his mind, now he could swear he still smelt the odor of them.

There were signs of damage that remained all over the bridge, but everything on it was operational again and that was what mattered. Most of the other repairs had been completed as well. The ship's one big weakness going back in was going to be her shields. The generators were just too badly burnt out to be fully repaired. The *Hellbringer*'s shield strength was only going to be around forty percent of it should be. That was a great deal more than either he or his engineering staff had expected based on their first estimates, but with the ship facing an entire fleet of Mechi warships, it made Captain Tanner very concerned about how any prolonged battle they found themselves in was going to go.

Ensign Sommers had detected a dropship distress beacon that was active on the surface of Wycarri Prime. The signal was weak, as the *Hellbringer* was still in Void space. Whether there was only one or signals coming in from every dropship that had left the *Hellbringer*'s bays, Captain Tanner knew they had to go back. He wasn't the type of officer who could live with leaving anyone behind. It was a choice that haunted him as he would be putting the entire ship at risk to save whoever was still alive, but he wasn't going to break his word.

On the upside, knowing the dropship's location, via the distress beacon signal, made it much easier to plan the *Hellbringer*'s return into the Wycarri system. He didn't have to go looking for the dropship. He knew exactly where it was. Nicholson, his helmsman, could plot a course into the system directly targeting the dropship's location and bring the massive carrier/battleship in right over its position. The question was whether the dropship was flight capable. If there was indeed only a sole dropship remaining, that meant things had likely gone as badly on the surface of Wycarri Prime as they had for the *Hellbringer* during the initial stages of the operation.

Captain Tanner had ordered the *Hellbringer*'s two remaining dropships prepped and ready to go in case the one on the planet's surface was unable to meet them in orbit. That was something he wouldn't know until the *Hellbringer* had dropped out of Void space and made contact with it. He wasn't fool enough to try to contact the dropship on the surface earlier than that. The Mechi might intercept any transmission he sent out of Void space, and if the bugs did that, his plan to rescue the dropship might go from suicidal to impossible. The Mechi forces in the system were already in a state of high alert because of the previous run on the planet and such a transmission might not only confirm for the bugs that the *Hellbringer* was indeed returning but also where it would be headed when it did.

"Mr. Nicholson, do you have our course laid in?" Captain Tanner asked.

"Aye, sir, I do," Nicholson answered from the *Hellbringer*'s helm.

Tanner's XO, Thorson, stood beside his command chair, frowning.

"Do you have something to say, Mr. Thorson?" Captain Tanner looked up at him.

"It's one dropship, sir," Thorson complained, "and we don't even know for sure that it's operational or if anyone is alive aboard it."

"I am well aware of those facts, Mr. Thorson." Captain Tanner lips curled into a frown of his own. "It doesn't change anything though. You know we have to go back."

"Understanding that we do and liking it are very different things, Captain," Thorson pointed out.

"Shields up, weapons online," Captain Tanner ordered.

"Shields up, weapons are powered and ready," Thorson confirmed.

Captain Tanner gave him a brisk nod. "Okay then. Mr. Nicholson, take us in."

The fabric of Void space ruptured around the *Hellbringer*. Captain Tanner felt the lurch of her transition as she dropped into the Wycarri system as close to achieving orbit around the bugs' homeworld as was safe for a vessel her size.

The *Hellbringer* appeared just outside of Wycarri Prime's gravity in a blinding flash of light. Captain Tanner smiled at the image of the Mechi fleet on the bridge's forward view screen. They had taken the bugs by surprise. The Mechi fleet was out of battle formation and a good deal of distance away from where the *Hellbringer* had entered real space. It was going to take time for the Mechi fleet to come about and engage her and the *Hellbringer* needed every second she could get.

"Launch fighters!" Captain Tanner shouted.

The massive carrier/battleship spat both of her fighter squadrons into space. They streaked out of her bays, racing towards the Mechi fleet already attempting to move to engage her. Captain Tanner hoped the fighters would buy the *Hellbringer* even more time and add to the state of chaos the Mechi fleet was already in.

"Fighters away!" Thorson reported.

"Maximum speed," Captain Tanner said, leaning forward in his command chair.

"Closing on Wycarri Prime now, sir," Nicholson assured him. "Maximum speed."

"Hail the dropship!" Captain Tanner ordered Sommers. "Get them moving to meet us if they're able."

"The dropship is attempting to make orbit, sir," Thorson cut in before Sommers could answer.

Captain Tanner let out an audible sigh of relief. Meeting the dropship would save them all time they desperately needed and keep him from needing to deploy the rescue dropships he had on standby in the *Hellbringer*'s bays.

"Run a full sensor sweep of the planet," Captain Tanner shouted at Murdock, his sensor tech. "We need to be sure that the approaching dropship is the only one left."

"Running sweep now, sir," Murdock answered.

"Make it fast," Captain Tanner growled.

****

Philip's fighter flew screaming from its launch tube. Elson's fighter swung in to form up with him as the *Hellbringer*'s two squadrons moved to engage the Mechi fleet. The engines of the Xera class fighter howled as Philip pushed them to their limits. The Mechi fleet was in disarray, but that was changing quickly.

The huge Mechi warships were turning to bring their primary missile tube and cannons towards the *Hellbringer*.

"Hit it hard, boys!" Philip heard Elson cry over the encrypted frequency the two squadrons were using.

The fighters fired a volley of ship-killer missiles into the Mechi fleet. Normally, it would have made sense to concentrate their fire and try to destroy or disable one of the Mechi warships, but this wasn't a normal battle. Their purpose was to keep the Mechi fleet from organizing fully against the *Hellbringer* for as long as they could.

The close-in defense systems of the Mechi warships swept most of the missiles aside before they ever reached the fleet. A handful did make it through. They impacted against the shields of the Mechi warships blossoming in orange-and-yellow explosions of bursting energy and flames.

"Yeehaw!" Elson shouted as the two squadrons of fighters reached the ranks of the warships in the wake of the missiles. The forward cannons of his Xera-class fighter spat streams of fire into the shields of a Mechi destroyer as Elson made a strafing run, flying over and along the length of its upper hull.

"Careful!" Philip warned him.

Elson's fighter broke hard to the right as a blast of return fire from one of the destroyer's cannons took a shot at it. The blast clipped the side of Elson's fighter and sent it spinning away from the destroyer. For a moment, Philip thought his friend wasn't going to be able to pull out of the spin before the next round of enemy fire came at him. All the Mechi warships were firing on the fighter squadrons now. Their great guns let loose hell into the

Void of space, moving on their turrets as they targeted the fighters attacking them.

Philip saw a fighter that had been sweeping in to engage a Mechi battleship break apart in a flash of fire and light. Pieces of the fighter spun away into space in the wake of the explosion that had ended it. The fighter wasn't the only one to go out in a blaze of glory. As the Mechi fleet really brought the sheer power of its weapons to bear on the fighter squadrons from the *Hellbringer*, half of them died within moments. There was no turning back though. Philip knew that he and the other pilots were committed to fight to the death.

Jerking the control stick of his fighter, Philip took it into a spin of its own as two Mechi ship-to-ship missiles came at it. As his fighter rolled, the two missiles streaked by him. Philip targeted them with his fighter's forward cannons, taking them out. Their explosions shook his fighter. A quick look at the data read out on his flight console told him that the shockwaves hadn't done any real damage to his craft. Philip knew he had to hold on. Whoever was aboard the dropship raising from the surface of the bug homeworld was counting on him. The crew of the *Hellbringer* was too. They both needed all the time he could buy for them.

No sooner had he recovered from the close call and righted his fighter on a course of the closest Mechi battleship when another missile locked onto his fighter and swooped in behind it. Philip flicked a switch on his control stick releasing the fighter's counter-measures. Flare-like projectiles launched from its rear towards the inbound missile. One by one, they detonated like flash bangs in the darkness of space, the last of them finally catching the missile with its blast. The Mechi missile vanished in an explosion that lit the Void behind his fighter.

"Mother ..." Philip started to curse, but the words froze on their way out of him as the battleship he was bearing down on opened fire with its forward cannons. He had just enough time to launch a final salvo of two ship-killer missiles at the great ship before the fire from the cannon met his fighter head on. Philip died instantly as an explosion of fire filled the cockpit of his fighter and the cannon's rounds tore through it.

****

An atmospheric Mechi fighter closed on Dropship 11 as Clayton pushed its engines beyond the redline. Clayton didn't give a crap if the engines burned out so long as they held on just long enough to reach orbit and the massive carrier/battleship that was waiting on Dropship 11 there. The dropship's sensor told him that the bug fighter was attempting to get a missile lock on it. Clayton knew he only had one round of counter-measures to launch in the dropship's defense when the bug in the cockpit of the closing fighter opened fire. He needed to hold on to it until the last possible moment and make sure he made it count.

The Mechi pilot had some talent, Clayton admitted to himself. Even as he pulled up and flipped the dropship over the inbound fighter to come in behind it, the Mechi pilot anticipated his action, twisting his fighter into an arc that took out of Clayton's line of fire. Dropship 11's forward cannons fired a barrage of rounds through the space the fighter had just occupied.

Clayton watched the Mechi fighter veering away from the dropship on the course it had taken to dodge his fire. He knew it would be back though. Clayton was surprised that only one Mechi fighter had engaged them thus far. There had to be more in route, but they would never reach the dropship in time to engage it.

An alarm lit up on the console in front of Clayton as the Mechi fighter completed its turn and came at Dropship 11 again. This time, the bug pilot wasn't waiting to get a solid lock. Two missiles flew from the fighter's wing-mounted launchers. He had no choice but to launch the counter-measures he had to block their path. Clayton launched them towards the missiles even as he rolled the dropship to port in an evasive maneuver. The counter-measures flew, creating a wall of flak between the inbound missiles and the dropship. The missiles plunged into it and died as they came.

"Yeah!" Clayton thumped the pilot console in victory as Dropship 11 continued to ascend. It broke through Wycarri Prime's atmosphere and into the darkness of space leaving the Mechi fighter behind.

"Republic dropship, this is Executive Officer Thorson of the *USS Hellbringer*," Clayton heard over his comm. "We have you on our sensors and moving to intercept you."

"On our way to you now, sir!" Clayton answered with a wide smile on his face.

Clayton was about to spin around in his seat to shout in the dropship's rear and let the others know they had made it when he felt a hand clamp onto his shoulder. He jumped, startled by the unexpected presence of someone else in the pilot compartment. Pain set his nerves on fire as the tip of a razor-like blade entered the side of his throat. The blade ran across the length of his throat from the side it entered to the other, silencing the cry that had been getting ready to erupt from his lips. Blood sprayed the dropship's forward window and the area in front of Clayton. As the blade withdrew from the flesh of his corpse, the hand holding him in place released its hold on him. Clayton slumped forward in his seat, his blood dripping onto the floor at his feet.

****

"Sir!" Thorson screamed at Captain Tanner.

Captain Tanner twisted in his command chair to look over at Thorson where the man had joined Ensign Ortega at the sensor station who had just started his duty shift as the *Hellbringer* had exited Void space and was still getting a handle on things.

"Our fighter squadrons have been eliminated," Thorson told him, concern and sadness in his voice.

"Understood," Captain Tanner snapped. He felt a pang of guilt at ordering those brave men and women to their death, but the squadrons had served their purpose. Thanks to their sacrifice, the Mechi fleet was only now beginning to concentrate its fire at the *Hellbringer* as the enemy ships moved to engage her.

"Fire at will," Captain Tanner ordered Herron, his weapons officer. "Hit them with everything we've got."

A volley of missiles left the *Hellbringer*'s launch tubes, targeting the lead ships of the Mechi fleet. Another followed seconds after it. Her portside cannons and railgun emplacements opened at the approaching bug ships as well. A handful of the Mechi vessels swerved away, engaging in evasive maneuvers, but the bulk of the enemy ships continued to barrel forward at the *Hellbringer*. Her electronic counter-measures filled the void between the two opposing sides with crackling static. Mechi missiles disrupted by them crashed into other missiles flying next to them, lighting up the darkness with rippling strips of explosions. The *Hellbringer*'s close-in defenses went to work on those that remained. Mechi missiles perished by the dozens as high-velocity rounds ripped through their ranks. It wasn't enough however.

The first of the Mechi missiles to make it through the hellish sea of explosions between the Mechi fleet and the *Hellbringer* hammered her shields. The solidified energy of the shields flared blue beneath the fury of the barrage colliding with them.

"Shields at twenty-four percent and continuing to drop, sir!" Thorson shouted. "We can't take this kind of beating much longer."

Captain Tanner prayed that they wouldn't need to.

"Dropship 11 has cleared Wycarri Prime's atmosphere, sir, and is on approach," Ensign Sommers shouted from the sensor station.

"Move to intercept," Captain Tanner ordered Nicholson.

Nicholson's fingers danced over the controls of the *Hellbringer*'s helm, adjusting the massive carrier/battleship's course towards the approaching dropship as it sped into space away from the bug homeworld.

The *Hellbringer* continued to pour fire at the Mechi fleet. Her cannons raked across the shields of all the closest Mechi ships, trying to collapse their shields. Several of the bug vessels were running without them, up already from the damage the *Hellbringer*'s fighters had rained upon them. One of the lead destroyers died a fiery death as a volley of missiles smashed into its unshielded hull. It exploded in a growing ball of orange-and-yellow fire that that reached out to lash at the shields of the two ships running along beside it.

Captain Tanner was just beginning to think they were going to make it out of the Wycarri system alive when things took a sharp nosedive and their luck ran out. The approaching Republic dropship zagged to starboard for no apparent reason.

"What the hell?" Captain Tanner snapped. "Hail that dropship and find out what in the holy hades its pilot thinks he's doing!"

"We've lost contact with the dropship, Captain," Ensign Sommers yelled back at him. "The pilot isn't responding to our hails."

Captain Tanner shot Thorson a sideways glance. The XO shrugged clearly as confused by the dropship's sudden erratic behavior as he was.

"Keep trying to make contact," Captain Tanner ordered Sommers. "Thorson, it looks like we may have to do this hard way."

"Aye, aye," Thorson answered him. "Bring the tractor beam generators online!"

Captain Tanner stabbed the comm. on his command chair, hailing engineering. "Chief, can you get us any more power to the engines?"

"Negative, sir!" the chief answered, "We're doing all we can just keep things holding together down here."

Another volley of Mechi missiles exploded against the *Hellbringer*'s shields. They collapsed under the force of the fury that splashed over them.

"Shields have collapsed, sir!" Thorson reported.

"Evasive maneuvers, pattern Alpha Tango 2," Captain Tanner ordered Nicholson.

The *Hellbringer* continued to inflict damage of her own against the ships of the Mechi fleet. A Mechi battleship, its shields already gone, veered to starboard, out of control, as the *Hellbringer*'s cannons lashed out, tearing open its hull. From the looks of it, the blast of fire had taken out the battleship's command bridge. Captain Tanner allowed himself a smile of pride at just how well his crew was performing given the intensity of the situation they were in. The battle was far from over, but at least they were alive and hanging on for the moment.

****

Aboard Dropship 11, Krellman had watched Shannon sling out of the straps of his safety harness. The little man had said he was heading up front to see if Clayton was having any issues with the repairs the two of them had made to the ship. Krellman had thought it odd, but Shannon was one of the oddest soldiers he had ever met in his career. The guy just didn't have a clue how to function socially. Krellman suspected there was more to Shannon's strangeness than just a lack of social skills. Shannon had, however, gotten the dropship flying, and that counted for a lot. Even so, Krellman's gut told him something was up.

Krellman eased out of his own safety harness and moved to follow Shannon into the pilot's compartment. He had felt the dropship leave the atmosphere of Wycarri Prime and knew that its inertial dampers would keep him being flung around too much no matter what crazy flying Clayton had to do now if the Mechi fleet surrounding the planet opened fire on them.

Making his way to the door that led into the dropship's pilot compartment, Krellman was utterly unprepared for what he saw through it. Shannon was standing behind Clayton's seat, covered in blood, holding a combat knife in his hand with a wide, almost feral grin stretching across his lips. Clayton's body was flopped over where it sat in the pilot seat, dripping red onto the floor.

"What the hell have you done?" Krellman shouted at Shannon.

The little man giggled. "I'm just having some fun, sniper boy. Don't worry. You're next."

Shannon lunged towards him, the blade of his knife lashing out. Krellman jumped backwards, narrowly avoiding it. Shannon was a lot faster than he looked, stronger too, Krellman found out. The swing of the knife had been a feint. Shannon's other hand smashed into the side of his head sending Krellman staggering. His ears rang and his vision blurred from the force of the blow he had been dealt. Krellman shook it off and sprang forward himself, hoping to catch the little man off balance. He did, ramming Shannon into the pilot console behind where he was standing. The two of them crashed into it. The little man cried out in pain as his back collided sharply with the console. He wasn't out of the fight however. Shannon brought up a knee into Krellman's stomach, knocking him away.

Krellman backed up, centering himself and assuming a combat stance. He wasn't a martial artist, but he knew how to fight. He had been in enough brawls during his time in the service to know how to fight dirty too. As Shannon came at him again, Krellman dropped, sweeping a leg under the little man's feet. Shannon crashed to the floor. The impact jarred the knife he clutched from his grasp. It clattered across the floor of the pilot compartment. Krellman leaped for it. His hand was almost on it when Shannon jumped onto his back, pulling his hair with one hand while the little man's other arm wound about his neck in an attempt to choke him. Krellman shook Shannon off, sending him crashing to the floor again.

"You're good, sniper boy." Shannon smiled up at him. "But not good enough."

Shannon drew another knife from a sheath hidden under the sleeve of his uniform and threw it at him. Krellman tried to fling himself to the side as the blade spun end over end through the air. His attempt to dodge saved his life, keeping the knife from burying its blade in his throat. He didn't escape it entirely though. The blade sunk into the meat of his left shoulder. Krellman let out a grunt of pain through gritted teeth as he jerked the blade free of his body. He held the blade, smeared with his own blood, at the ready as the little man got to his feet.

"Why did you do it, Shannon?" Krellman demanded. "There was no reason to kill Clayton. He was one of us!"

"You just don't get it, sniper boy," Shannon cackled. "Killing is what I do. Human, Mechi, whatever. It doesn't matter. All races bleed and all life dies."

"You've killed us both," Krellman told Shannon. Without Clayton to fly it, the dropship was continuing along the last course Clayton had it on, its engines at full power. Through its forward window, Krellman could see the massive battle raging around it.

The *Hellbringer* was engaged against an entire fleet of Mechi warships, and the bugs looked to be kicking the crap out of it. Its shields had to be down because explosions rippled along its side as Mechi missiles blew gaping holes in its hull.

Shannon threw his hands wide, laughing. "Like I said, we all die. We just have to try to have what fun we can in the time allotted to us."

Krellman knew he had to deal with Shannon quickly. If he could stop the little man from being a threat maybe, just maybe, he could figure out how to fly the dropship in the direction of the *Hellbringer* to give the carrier/battleship a better chance of picking them up.

"Your move, sniper," Shannon suddenly growled at him as if reading his thoughts.

Krellman and Shannon circled each other in the confined space of pilot compartment. Krellman finally took a swing at the little man. The blade of the knife slashed over Shannon's head as the little man ducked his attack and threw his weight against Krellman's stomach, tackling him. Krellman crashed into the wall, his breath knocked from his lungs by the impact as Shannon struggled to wrest the knife from his hand. Krellman held onto it with all the strength he could muster. The two of them wrestled viciously as Krellman fought loose from where Shannon pressed him against the compartment's wall. The little man's face rose up towards Krellman's throat. He screamed as Shannon sunk his teeth into the flesh there and ripped away a chunk of it. Of all the little man's craziness, Krellman hadn't expected such a savage attack. The little man got the upper hand in their melee, swinging him forward to go sprawling onto the floor. Krellman managed to keep his grasp on the knife and tried to get up. As he did so, one of Shannon's boots met his face. Krellman blinked in pain and heard the crunch of bone as he felt his nose break. Thudding back to the floor, Krellman rolled away from Shannon.

"Not so tough now, are you, sniper?" Shannon gloated, closing in on him.

"Tougher than you," Krellman said, grabbing one of Shannon's legs and pulling it from under him. Shannon thumped to the floor next to where he lay. Krellman rolled over on top of the little man raising the knife to plunge it into him. Shannon stopped him though, thrusting a balled-up fist upwards into the center of his throat. Krellman lost the advantage he had gained as Shannon threw him to the side and sprang to his feet again. The little man stood over him, laughing.

"You snipers are so smug and self-assured," Shannon told him. "After you're dead, I think I am going to teach you a thing or two about humility."

Krellman didn't even know what the little man meant by that and didn't care. He had no intention of dying. He swung the knife outward in an arc at Shannon's legs. The little man easily sidestepped the attack just as Krellman had expected him to. Krellman used the moment to spring to his feet and run towards the dropship's rear compartment. Shannon came charging after him.

"You're running now." Shannon laughed. "The great and mighty sniper Krellman on the run from little old me."

Krellman spun around to meet Shannon, the barrel of his rifle that he had just retrieved leveled at the maniac's chest. "Bye now." Krellman grinned as he squeezed the weapon's trigger. The rifle bucked in his hands at it fired. Shannon's chest exploded into a mass of gore as the high-powered round shattered his ribs and sent the little man sprawling backwards. Krellman stood there, rifle in his hands, staring at Shannon's corpse and the pool of red growing around it on the floor.

"Frag you," Krellman muttered.

Stumbling into the pilot's compartment, Krellman shoved Clayton's corpse from the pilot seat and collapsed into it. He wiped smeared blood from his lips with the backside of his hand as he looked over the dropship's helm controls, trying to figure out how to operate them, and activated the comm.

"This is Dropship 11 to the *Hellbringer*," he said. "Our pilot is dead. Request pick up. Over."

"This is Captain Tanner," a strained voice answered him. "We're in route for pick up now. Be ready. It's going to be rough."

"Yes, sir," Krellman answered. All he could do was wait and pray whatever Captain Tanner was planning worked. His fate was out of his hands, and he would either live or die as the good Lord willed.

****

The *Hellbringer* was taking heavy fire. Thorson had reported breaches all over hull, spanning numerous decks. She was holding together, if barely. Captain Tanner knew she couldn't do it much longer though. The comm. station had blown out again just after contact with Dropship 11 had been established. Thankfully, they were able to let whoever was alive over there know that they were coming. Now everything all came down to one all or nothing maneuver.

"Nicholson," Captain Tanner called his helmsman.

"Sir!" Nicholson snapped.

"Intercept that dropship now!" Captain Tanner ordered.

Nicholson stared at him, hesitating. "Sir, that will take us directly towards the approaching Mechi fleet."

"He's right," Thorson echoed. "I'm not sure we can survive that kind of charge."

"Do it!" Captain Tanner growled at Nicholson. "Or give your station over to someone who will."

"Yes, sir!" Nicholson nodded.

The *Hellbringer* shifted her course to intercept the dropship. It put her on a collision course with the Mechi. Her few still-functioning missile tubes fired rapidly, expending the entirety of their magazines at the bug fleet. Her forward cannons joined them, blazing away at full power. Two bug destroyers died from the fury of the barrage and the lead Mechi battleship took a heavy beating that crippled its forward weapons. The shrapnel from the exploding destroyers helped to block a portion of the missiles the ships behind them spat at the *Hellbringer*. None of the Mechi vessels were targeting the dropship. It was too small and unarmed to be a threat to them. It meant everything to Captain Tanner and the crew of the *Hellbringer* however.

"Engage tractor beam!" Captain Tanner leaned forward in his command chair, screaming at Nicholson.

Nicholson stabbed a button on the controls in front of him. He let the ship's computer do the targeting for him. The tractor beam snagged the dropship, reeling it in toward the *Hellbringer*'s open, portside bay.

The bridge shook as a Mechi missile made it through the *Hellbringer*'s ECMS and close-in defenses. The *Hellbringer* titled sideways in space. Nicholson fought savagely to get her under control.

"That one just blew the hell out of our aft section, sir!" Thorson wailed. "Another hit like that and it's over for us. Our structural integrity has been compromised to near the point of collapse captain!"

"Is the dropship aboard?" Captain Tanner demanded, ignoring Thorson's panic.

"She's in the hangar, sir!" Nicholson answered.

"Then get us out of here, Mr. Nicholson!" Captain Tanner shouted, his knuckles white from the hold he had on the arms of his command chair.

"Engaging Void drive now, sir!" Nicholson barked back at him.

A final missile rammed into the *Hellbringer* as space distorted around her, and she disappeared from the Wycarri system in a blinding flash of light.

She hung in the red empty expanse of Void space as Captain Tanner yelled, "Damage report!"

"That last hit took our sub-Void engines offline, sir," Thorson told him. "I've got a report coming in for twenty-two crewmen dead in engineering alone."

The XO's causality report took the edge off the sheer relief Captain Tanner was feeling. There were so many dead. Whoever was aboard the dropship better be worth it, he thought, and then turned in his seat to grin at Thorson. "We made it."

"That we did, sir." Thorson returned his smile.

"I want repairs started at once on any systems that can be attended to while we're on the move," Captain Tanner ordered. "Mr. Nicholson, lay a course for Earth, best possible speed."

"Aye, sir," Nicholson answered him happily.

Captain Tanner slumped, exhausted, in his command chair. Despite all he and his crew had suffered, they had lived through it. It spoke volumes about the quality of crew that he commanded. When the *Hellbringer* was fully repaired, which would likely take weeks in a proper space dock, the Mechi would still be out, waiting. Captain Tanner promised himself that he would make the bugs pay for each and every one of the men and women who had died in the Wycarri system. For now though, he was content just to be alive and on his way home at last.

Epilogue

Krellman had been debriefed at least six times before they had allowed him to leave the orbiting defense station for Earth. The powers that be had a difficult time accepting that someone had fooled the psych evaluations required for all military personnel to the point that Shannon had done. The thought of having allowed a serial killer into their ranks was disturbing. A search into Shannon's background turned up murders he had committed through the colony worlds of the Republic before assuming his final identity and joining up with the colonial marines. His real name had been Daniel Stark. Krellman didn't give a crap. He was just happy that the bastard was dead and that was enough. His crimes had been ended by a point-blank, explosive round to the chest. Given the murders that Shannon, or Daniel it seemed, committed, there were no charges brought against him. If anything, instead of being punished, Krellman was a full-fledged hero in the eyes of the Republic's civilians and greener recruits of the colonial marines. The propaganda machine of the press made him turned him into one. "The sole survivor of Operation: Hive Strike!" the press had labeled him. A picture of him in full combat gear adorned the colonial marines' recruiting posters. Really, all he had done was survive. It was as simple as that, no matter how the press played it up.

After the debriefings, Captain Tanner of the *Hellbringer* had paid him a personal visit. Tanner had wanted to meet him. Krellman knew he would have wanted the same in Tanner's position. The captain had sacrificed a great deal to make sure he had come home. Krellman thanked him, but the words seemed hollow and unable to truly express the level of gratitude he felt. The two of them had shared a drink before Captain Tanner had finally left to return to overseeing the repairs that were in progress to the *Hellbringer.*

Rumor had it that the Mechi were preparing to launch a massive counter-offensive against the Republic. Krellman had been offered an honorary discharge with full retirement benefits, but he had declined it. His place was on the front line against the bugs. He was a born killer just like Shannon, though he killed for the defense of Earth and its colony worlds, not his own pleasure.

Still, the line between the two of them was thinner than Krellman liked to dwell on.

The shuttle he was aboard touched down just outside the gates of the gigantic, military cemetery built to honor those lost in the Mechi war. Krellman walked through it, searching, until he found the grave marker erected for Gunter. Kneeling beside it, he wiped at his eyes, fighting to keep the tears welling up in his eyes from showing.

"I'm sorry, Gunter," Krellman whispered to the empty grave. "You were the only real friend I ever had."

The only answer he received was the wind howling through the trees that surrounded the vast field of the dead. Krellman rose to his feet and saluted Gunter's grave marker. "Oorah, brother," Krellman said, and again more loudly, "Oorah."

Krellman looked at the dark clouds gathering in the sky above him. A gentle rain began to fall from the heavens hiding his tears as they finally began to flow. He lingered at Gunter's grave until the shuttle pilot called out for him to tell him it was time to go. Krellman had to be onboard the *USS Juggernaut* by o'sixteen hundred hours. The *Juggernaut* was leaving the Sol system to intercept the Mechi fleet that had now been confirmed to be on its way towards the Republic's outer colony worlds.

Krellman ran to the shuttle where the pilot was waiting on him.

"You ready to go sir?" the pilot asked.

Nodding, Krellman smiled at him. "It's time to kill some bugs."

END

Author Bio

Eric S Brown is the author of numerous book series including the Bigfoot War series, the Kaiju Apocalypse series (with Jason Cordova), the Crypto-Squad series (with Jason Brannon), the Homeworld series (With Tony Faville and Jason Cordova), the Jack Bunny Bam series, and the A Pack of Wolves series. Some of his stand alone books include War of the Worlds plus Blood Guts and Zombies, Kraken, World War of the Dead, The Last Fleet, Sasquatch Lake, Kaiju Armageddon, Megalodon, Megalodons, and Megalodon Apocalypse to name only a few. His short fiction has been published hundreds of times in the small press in beyond including markets like the Onward Drake and Black Tide Rising anthologies from Baen Books, the Grantville Gazette, the SNAFU Military horror anthology series, and Walmart World magazine. He has done the novelizations for such films as Boggy Creek: The Legend is True (Studio 3 Entertainment) and The Bloody Rage of Bigfoot (Great Lake films). The first book of his Bigfoot War series was adapted into a feature film by Origin Releasing in 2014. Werewolf Massacre at Hell's Gate was the second his books to be adapted into film in 2015. In addition to his fiction, Eric also writes an award winning comic book news column entitled "Comics in a Flash." Eric lives in North Carolina with his wife and two children where he continues to write tales of the hungry dead, blazing guns, and the things that lurk in the woods.

CHECK OUT OTHER GREAT SCIENCE FICTION BOOKS

IN PERPETUITY
by Jake Bible

For two thousand years, Earth and her many colonies across the galaxy have fought against the Estelian menace. Having faced overwhelming losses, the CSC has instituted the largest military draft ever, conscripting millions into the battle against the aliens. Major Bartram North has been tasked with the unenviable task of coordinating the military education of hundreds of thousands of recruits and turning them into troops ready to fight and die for the cause.

As Major North struggles to maintain a training pace that the CSC insists upon, he realizes something isn't right on the Perpetuity. But before he can investigate, the station dissolves into madness brought on by the physical booster known as pharma. Unfortunately for Major North, that is not the only nightmare he faces- an armada of Estelian warships is on the edge of the solar system and headed right for Earth!

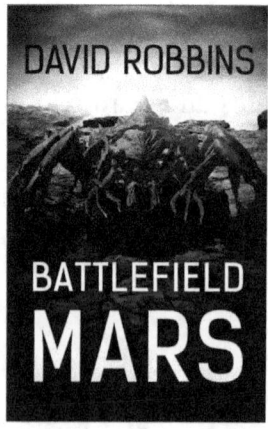

BATTLEFIELD MARS
by David Robbins

Several centuries into the future, Earth has established three colonies on Mars. No indigenous life has been discovered, and humankind looks forward to making the Red Planet their own.

Then 'something' emerges out of a long-extinct volcano and doesn't like what the humans are doing.

Captain Archard Rahn, United Nations Interplanetary Corps, tries to stem the rising tide of slaughter. But the Martians are more than they seem, and it isn't long before Mars erupts in all-out war.

CHECK OUT OTHER GREAT
SCIENCE FICTION BOOKS

MAUSOLEUM 2069
by Rick Jones

Political dignitaries including the President of the Federation gather for a ceremony onboard Mausoleum 2069. But when a cloud of interstellar dust passes through the galaxy and eclipses Earth, the tenants within the walls of Mausoleum 2069 are reborn and the undead begin to rise. As the struggle between life and death onboard the mausoleum develops, Eriq Wyman, a one-time member of a Special ops team called the Force Elite, is given the task to lead the President to the safety of Earth. But is Earth like Mausoleum 2069? A landscape of the living dead? Has the war of the Apocalypse finally begun? With so many questions there is only one certainty: in space there is nowhere to run and nowhere to hide.

RED CARBON
by D.J. Goodman

Diamonds have been discovered on Mars.

After years of neglect to space programs around the world, a ruthless corporation has made it to the Red Planet first, establishing their own mining operation with its own rules and laws, its own class system, and little oversight from Earth. Conditions are harsh, but its people have learned how to make the Martian colony home.

But something has gone catastrophically wrong on Earth. As the colony leaders try to cover it up, hacker Leah Hartnup is getting suspicious. Her boundless curiosity will lead her to a horrifying truth: they are cut off, possibly forever. There are no more supplies coming. There will be no more support. There is no more mission to accomplish. All that's left is one goal: survival.

CHECK OUT OTHER GREAT SCIENCE FICTION BOOKS

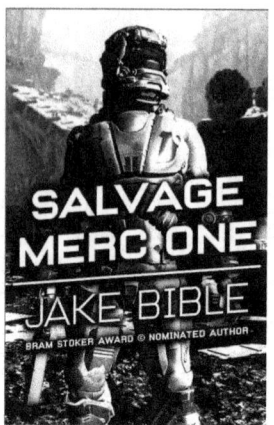

SALVAGE MERC ONE
by **Jake Bible**

Joseph Laribeau was born to be a Marine in the Galactic Fleet. He was born to fight the alien enemies known as the Skrang Alliance and travel the galaxy doing his duty as a Marine Sergeant. But when the War ended and Joe found himself medically discharged, the best job ever was over and he never thought he'd find his way again.

Then a beautiful alien walked into his life and offered him a chance at something even greater than the Fleet, a chance to serve with the Salvage Merc Corp.

Now known as Salvage Merc One Eighty-Four, Joe Laribeau is given the ultimate assignment by the SMC bosses. To his surprise it is neither a military nor a corporate salvage. Rather, Joe has to risk his life for one of his own. He has to find and bring back the legend that started the Corp.

SERENGETI
by J.B. Rockwell

It was supposed to be an easy job: find the Dark Star Revolution Starships, destroy them, and go home. But a booby-trapped vessel decimates the Meridian Alliance fleet, leaving Serengeti—a Valkyrie class warship with a sentient AI brain—on her own; wrecked and abandoned in an empty expanse of space. On the edge of total failure, Serengeti thinks only of her crew. She herds the survivors into a lifeboat, intending to sling them into space. But the escape pod sticks in her belly, locking the cryogenically frozen crew inside.

Then a scavenger ship arrives to pick Serengeti's bones clean. Her engines dead, her guns long silenced, Serengeti and her last two robots must find a way to fight the scavengers off and save the crew trapped inside her.